PENELOPE LIVELY

Spiderweb

VIKING

VIKING

Published by the Penguin Group
Penguin Books Ltd, 27 Wrights Lane, London w8 5tz, England
Penguin Putnam Inc., 375 Hudson Street, New York, New York 10014, USA
Penguin Books Australia Ltd, Ringwood, Victoria, Australia
Penguin Books Canada Ltd, 10 Alcorn Avenue, Toronto, Ontario, Canada m4v 3b2
Penguin Books (NZ) Ltd, Private Bag 102902, NSMC, Auckland 10, New Zealand

Penguin Books Ltd, Registered Offices: Harmondsworth, Middlesex, England

First published 1998
3 5 7 9 10 8 6 4

Set in 11.5/14pt Monotype Garamond by Intype London Ltd
Printed in Great Britain by Clays Ltd, St Ives plc

A CIP catalogue record for this book is available from the British Library
isbn 0–670–86906–6

Chapter One

The west of England was once remote, inaccessible and inconvenient. Somerset, Devon, Cornwall. Country cousins lived there, whose uncouth accents provoked ridicule when they came up to town. It was picturesque, in those parts, but barbarous, and to be avoided except for purposes of absentee landownership.

All that has changed, except that the place remains scenic – though perhaps rather less so. The three counties are now quite close to the centre of things – to Birmingham and Liverpool and Manchester and London. Consequently the balance of the country shifts, come high summer. The north and the centre tip down into the west in such concentration that when there is no longer a single car-park space left, or boarding-house bed, or vacant bay on a caravan site, they have to put up the 'Cornwall Full' sign on the county boundary.

The natives of the West Country are still there and they continue to speak with distinctive voices, but they are joined now by many others – those who have drifted west and slotted themselves into the local economy, those who have ended up there in remembrance of an agreeable summer holiday.

Ancestry and happenstance divide the population, today –

people who have always been there and people who came there fortuitously. For these last, fortune can serve up some strange conjunctions.

North Somerset Herald

A CHARACTER DETACHED COTTAGE occupying a peaceful situation a mile from Kingston Florey village and with excellent views in a southerly direction.

Good-sized living-room with inglenook, kitchen/breakfast-room, bathroom, bedroom, bedroom/boxroom. Pleasant gardens to front and rear.

Mains water and electricity. Septic tank drainage.

DIRECTIONS: The property lies off the B4167, going east from Kingston Florey. Access is by way of the lane to the right half a mile beyond the village (with sign indicating T. G. Hiscox, agricultural contractor).

T. G. Hiscox
Agricultural engineer and contractor

Grass silage	Agri-pac bagging system
Muck spreading	Ploughing crawler or 4 w/d
Power harrowing	Maize drilling and harvesting
Combine harvesting	Mole draining and subsoiling
Drilling	Heavy discing
Repairs and servicing	

Richard Faraday to Stella Brentwood

Dear Stella,

I have cast an eye over the property advertisements in the local paper, as requested, and believe I may have come up with a possibility. Particulars enclosed. It meets your specifications in various ways – absence of busy adjacent road, good rural views. The place is situated in a quiet backwater – a scatter of nearby cottages, one farm, and at the far end of the lane there are the bungalow and repair yard of an agricultural contractor – at some considerable distance and therefore not a potential source of noise or nuisance. I have had a scout around the area and found everything most agreeable.

Since my previous letter a few thoughts have occurred. I am sure that you will find these parts as congenial for retirement as I do. I feel, though, that I should warn you there are aspects of life down here which you might find it difficult to come to terms with, if you do decide to follow this through. Forewarned is forearmed!

RAIN: you are drawn to this area by the glories of the landscape (I take it). Relatively mild, yes (very little frost or snow – influence of the sea), but wet. Adjust your expectations accordingly.

SOCIAL SERVICES: this is a rural area – hospitals and such are spread thin. Expect to have to drive twenty miles to get your teeth seen to – that sort of thing. But of course you will have considerable experience of this on your various field trips. I merely mention the matter.

ENTERTAINMENT: as above.

DRIVING: You will be doing a lot of this (arising out of the preceding points) – mostly in narrow lanes which do not allow two vehicles to pass except at gateways or deliberately constructed indentations in the hedgebanks. The local convention is that the vehicle going uphill is the one to do the backing. On the flat, it is a question of staring down the opposition, if equidistant from a passing place. Tractors, milk tankers and agricultural suppliers always have right of way. I advise a small, manoeuvrable car. I drive a VW Golf.

HUNTING: both fox and stag. An entrenched local tradition.

Adverse comment can provoke ill feeling, and worse. I strongly advise a policy of silent neutrality, whatever your natural reactions may be.

RELIGIOUS PRACTICE: I seem to recall that you are agnostic, but I would suggest, with all respect, that you stretch a point and attend Sunday Matins, at least on occasion. You will thus establish yourself in the community and make useful contacts. It is a question of social expediency rather than a spiritual commitment.

Let me say again that I am very pleased that you may settle in these parts. I know that Nadine would have been delighted to think that her oldest friend would be my neighbour, so to speak. Please let me know if there is anything further over which I can be of use.

Yours,
    Richard

North Somerset Herald

ITEMS FOR SALE: Livestock and Poultry
Free range eggs, rabbits (live & frozen oven-ready), ducks, young cockerels from £5.50. K. Hiscox, T. G. Hiscox, Agricultural Engineers, Kingston Florey.

Women's Institute Reports

KINGSTON FLOREY: The new president, Mrs Joyce Williams, welcomed twenty-six members and friends. Mr Paul Hampton spoke on bee-keeping and its products, which was very interesting. After the meeting members were able to buy honey and candles made by his bees. Refreshments were served and the retiring president Mrs Pleydell and secretary Mrs Davies were thanked for all their hard work over the last three years and presented with a rose bush each.

Live Music

The Mayfair Bar, Minehead
Thurs: Blossom Sisters and Crazy Jane
Fri: The Devils Incarnate
Sat: Hullabaloo

Foxhampton Barbarians RFC
Under 17s Disco Rave at Foxhampton Rugby Club
Friday 4 May, 7.30–11.00 p.m.

Hunting

Clarkton Farm Meet. Mr and Mrs Apsley kindly entertained all comers. Hounds moved off to draw Pinner Wood, where they found and went away across Hallows Farm, down Clacombe to Parkers Plantation, over to Wester Lea, down Mapley and ran swiftly to Lannersmead, where he went to ground. Hounds were taken back to Eastcombe, where they drew with no luck, cast down through Candon Water and up on to the heath where a fox was found. Hounds ran well in a circuit back to Eastcombe, where the scent was lost. Hounds found again in the quarry but checked almost at once, cast on over Shapcott, into Burnley Wood and round Bittersedge without finding again, so the day ended.

It is possible, within this deeply rural landscape, to play golf, to go hang-gliding or moto-cross racing, or to indulge in a bout of ten-pin bowling or skittles any day of the week. You can sail, cycle, walk, ride. You could also take up country dancing or enjoy change-ringing or go fishing. The visitor is richly indulged and may choose between castles, abbeys, stately homes, gardens of national repute, scenic railways, tropiquaria, farm parks, country life museums, trout fisheries. There are fifteen hunts within a radius of thirty miles, including harriers and beagles.

You might think that the entire place is given over to the purveying of leisure activities. This is not so. Real life continues here, beneath the surface gloss of brown signs inviting a departure from the main roads carrying glittery lines of cars which slice their way though the green quilt of fields and hills. People are still growing things and selling them and providing one another with services and necessities. Most of them spend much of their time in one place, contemplating the same view, locked in communion with those they see every day. For some, this is a stranglehold; others are more fortunate. It all depends on perspective.

Chapter Two

The man and the two boys watched her come out of the bungalow. They saw her slam the door, march down the path, get into the car, roar the engine. The boys noted the set of her mouth, the swagger in her step, the deliberate din of door and accelerator. It could get their insides churning when she was like that, but this time they were in the clear.

Michael said, 'Going to Carter's, isn't she?'

Their father nodded.

The car shot off, spraying dirt. They watched it belt away and turn into the lane that led to the main road.

'Give Carter an earful, I bet,' said Peter. 'Stupid bugger don't know what's coming to him.'

Carter had a business selling animal feed. He'd sent one of his men over last night asking again for cash for a delivery made six weeks ago. She wasn't paying because she said the delivery was a sack short. She'd have to find another supplier, but that wouldn't bother her. Rather that and be one up on Carter.

'Was the sacks one short?' he said after a moment.

Their father shrugged. 'Dunno. Could be.'

'Stupid bugger,' Peter said again. 'He can't do nothing, can he, if she won't pay?'

Ted Hiscox grinned. 'He'll say he's taking her to court, but he won't. Too much trouble, in the long run. He'll want to get her off his back, anyway.'

The boys stood there, thinking of her. Their thoughts ran parallel, as usual, and both knew this, so they did not even need to look at one another to be in accord. They thought of her bawling the man out at his own depot, in front of his men and other customers and whoever. She'd go on as long as it suited her. When she came back she'd be pleased as anything, riding high, in a good mood that would last the rest of the day. So Carter had done them a favour.

Ted Hiscox turned towards the repair shed. 'I got a job over by Treborough. Get those tyres moved out of the way before I get back.'

When he had gone the boys went behind the shed to the place they'd made, a scoop in the hedge with a roof of corrugated iron. They sat in there and smoked, as near to easy as they could ever be, knowing that she was miles away. For an hour or so. They were fourteen and fifteen, short, stocky, silent boys with shaggy black hair who seldom spoke except to each other because they knew the rest of the world to be against them. They had been in collusion all their lives, embattled together against everything. Against her, first and last.

The younger boy, Peter, said, 'Where'll she get feed from now?'

'Plenty of places.'

That was it, you could always move on. That was what she said herself – if someone tried to put one over you, then you gave them the shove. It's each for himself in this world, she said, you'd better remember that or you'll get nowhere. They remembered. They watched her and remembered.

Both of them wondered now if there'd really been a sack short. Not that it mattered one way or the other.

Stella Brentwood, looking out of the window of her kitchen, saw a red car go past along the lane, driven rather too fast. She did not much register either car or driver, since her mind at that moment was on other things. She was concerned with various needs and deficiencies within this new home: a lack of storage space, a dripping tap, a recalcitrant radiator. She was making a list, but the making of the list had been interrupted by a phone call, and now the phone call had distracted her further. By the time the red car had gone past she was no longer thinking of taps or radiators but had been pitched into another time and place which seemed suddenly more vivid and more reliable than this unfamiliar view of greenery, pink earth and the long slack lines of hills.

When Stella was twenty-one her best friend's recently acquired lover took the most tremendous shine to her. He did little to conceal this and the best friend soon cottoned on. She tackled Stella in the ladies' loo of the pub where a gang of them, the lover included, were having a few drinks before going on to a bottle party in someone's flat which would probably last all night and at which much would be got up to.

'Hands off,' said Nadine, powdering her nose. 'He's mine.'

There had never been such talk between them before. Nadine meant business. She had not had much luck with men and saw this as her last chance. Marriage was taken seriously, back then, and was an essential move, even for a girl with an Oxford degree in history.

'I don't want him,' said Stella. 'He's not my type.'

'I dare say not, but you seem to be his.' Nadine brushed

powder flecks from her black jersey bat-wing top and shook out the turquoise circular felt skirt. She tightened her three-inch-wide belt by another notch. 'So hands off, if you don't mind.'

Stella considered. This moment of effortless power was rather enjoyable, even between old friends.

'James Stanway is coming to the party,' said Nadine. 'You've always had a thing about him.'

'It's peaked,' said Stella. 'But I'll look around and see what else there is.'

They inspected their reflections in the pock-marked mirror. They knew everything about each other, from political and spiritual views through food fads and fashion tastes to the details of their menstrual cycles.

'Your bra strap shows a bit,' said Nadine. 'Is that scent Muguet des Bois or Mitsouko?'

They gathered up their possessions and bounced back to the steamy clamour of their friends, who were setting up a kitty for the purchase of bottles of cheap plonk. Presently they all surged off to the party, which by the small hours degenerated into a semi-darkness strident with gramophone records that kept getting stuck, and heaving bodies on floor and sofas. Stella heaved half-heartedly for a while with someone she hardly knew, who took her home in a taxi but turned out to be too sloshed to pay the fare. Nadine had somehow kept possession of the lover all night, though wearing a strained expression. Within months he had cleared off and a year later Nadine married Richard Faraday, who had taken the Civil Service exam and was starting at the Home Office.

'Hang your hat on a pension,' said Stella. 'Incidentally he doesn't fancy me at all. I don't think he even likes me.'

Nadine giggled. She was heady with relief and excitement. There was going to be a proper wedding – no cut-price registry office do – and a two-bedroom flat in Fulham.

'You next,' she said benevolently.

By then they were twenty-three. Getting on in years, almost over the hill. If you were going to have children, said Nadine, you had to do it well before you were thirty, or you got incredibly fat and your insides went to pot entirely. She should make it nicely – two babies at least. By that time the Fulham flat would have been traded in for a house in Richmond, or maybe out in the country. But she was worried about Stella. After a further couple of years the benevolent concern turned to serious anxiety.

'Listen,' she said. 'Apart from anything else, being married means sex whenever you like and not being scared all the time about getting pregnant.' Nadine was by now extremely pregnant. 'All those years counting the calendar . . . I've forgotten what it was like.'

Contrary to popular belief, the young of the fifties had as vibrant a sex life as those of the nineties. They simply made less fuss about it. Stella and Nadine had both had some anxious moments with the calendar.

'I'll have to take my chance,' said Stella. It was not clear if she referred to her prospects of getting pregnant inadvertently or the effect on her figure and her insides of doing so too late.

Nadine gave her a cautionary look. The word spinster was still around back then – at its last gasp, admittedly. It hung between them, unspoken.

'Maybe I'll remain single,' said Stella, ahead of her time semantically and perhaps in other ways.

'What about sex?'

'I don't see that as a great problem.' Again, it was not quite clear what Stella meant.

'Men go for you,' said Nadine sternly, as though this created some sort of obligation.

'Oh, I rather go for them, too.'

Nadine sighed, rolled her eyes equivocally and folded her hands on her swelling stomach. She wore a voluminous pinafore dress. In Stella's opinion, marriage had flung her friend into a premature matronhood that seemed like some smug assumption of the veil. Nadine, on the other hand, saw Stella as perversely embracing a future of promiscuity and ultimate solitude. This disparity of vision was to prompt a gradual distancing between the two of them. Monthly meetings would give way to an occasional exchange of letters and eventually to the ritual Christmas card.

'How is Richard?' said Stella, moving on to safer ground.

Richard, today, was a mere fifteen miles away and was perhaps also briefly deflected to other times by his phone conversation with Stella. It had been a slightly stilted conversation. Stella had been conscious that she was in his debt on account of the information about the cottage and should make some definite social overture. Richard had rung to ask if her removal had gone smoothly. He had seemed to scrape around determinedly for things to say. A rather stiff man, she remembered, always apparently on his best behaviour, perhaps because he knew of no other kind. In the end she had invited him over for lunch in a couple of days' time.

She had forgotten that Richard was living in the West Country until his Christmas card had arrived, bleak with its solitary name in a neat, constricted hand. She remembered Nadine's flowing scrawl. And noticed, too, the postmark. She was favouring that area herself as a place in which to settle. The card and the postmark had tipped the balance. She wrote to Richard asking him to look at estate agents' advertisements for her.

'I hope the new home is up to expectations,' Richard had said just now, and for an instant she hadn't understood what on earth he was on about. Whose home? Ah – her home, of course. This was what she now had, apparently. And must set to and play the part. Nest. Embellish. Fix rogue radiators, fit washers to taps.

She had lived, time was, in a house made of dried mud, in a straw hut, in various tents. In bed-sitters and flats over corner shops or at the top of high-rise buildings or slotted into nineteenth-century mansions. In a stone croft on an island and in a room over the coffee shop in a Greek mountain village. She had not perceived these places as homes, though each had in its way become important to her. She could still revisit them, in her head, could tour the fittings and fixtures. Her bed in the mud house had a thick woven red cover with a zig-zag pattern in black. On the wall of the flat above a greengrocer's shop in Liverpool there hung a reproduction Degas of ballet dancers. The yellow oilcloth on the kitchen table of the stone croft was rubbed and cracked with age. These objects operated as a personal mnemonic system, but a random one. No logical progression ran from one to another: they were simply there, in full colour and with precise detail, serving as hitching posts and as prompts.

A social anthropologist lives over the shop, in a professional sense as well as sometimes in a literal one. Field-work is not an occupation conducive to family life, as Stella had had occasion to note. Marriages tended to break up when couples were confronted with the raw choice of extended separation or intense proximity under taxing conditions. In her trade, you travelled most fruitfully if you travelled alone. And it helped it you were footloose and singularly unfettered by personal possessions.

But now she owned a house. This house, this home. An entanglement that was causing her some unease as she confronted the implications. This is where she would now live, not just for weeks or months but for the foreseeable future. For years.

Her last job had been at a Midlands university. And where are you going to live? her colleagues had asked, as the final months ticked away, the countdown to the end of the summer term that would mark also this eerie shift from employment to statutory leisure. At first she had ignored the question. Then she had contemplated the prospect of continuing to live in the inner-city flat with nothing to recommend it but its convenient closeness to her department. Then she started looking at the atlas.

Thus, the cottage. She had seen at once that it would do, that, as Richard Faraday said, it met all her stipulated requirements. She couldn't be bothered to trawl estate agents in case something marginally better lay around the corner. She bought it.

And now she felt no proprietorial surge, no glow of ownership. She would have to get more furniture, to build bookshelves. Of more immediate importance, she needed to discover this place, to do the sort of things she had always done in new surroundings. Move about, observe, listen. Without notebook or tape recorder but simply for her own interest, because she could no longer imagine any other way of living.

The world is out there, richly stocked and inviting observation.

She was sixty-five, apparently. This totemic number had landed her here. Having spent much time noting and inter-preting complex rites of passage in alien societies, she now found herself subject to one of the implacable rules of her own: stop working, get old.

In other societies the likes of her would be variously seen as valuable repositories of knowledge, as objects of pity and respect, or as economic encumbrances ripe for disposal. Exempt from such extremes, she could define her own pos-ition. She could be as she wished, do as she liked.

She had plans. There were articles that she intended to write, for the journals of her trade. She would keep her hand in professionally. But she would branch out, also. Read with luxurious eclecticism, pander to ignorance, learn about things of which she knew nothing.

And I will get a dog, she thought suddenly. I have always liked animals and there has never been an opportunity. A dog is appropriate, in a place like this, it would serve as a credential. I live here now — this is the end of the line, the last stop.

The prospect began to be interesting. She turned from the window and looked around her: at her own possessions which invited arrangement — books to be unpacked, pictures to be hung — at the fireplace for which she must find logs, the windows that needed curtains.

Stella turned from the window and went to the telephone, to rally plumbers and carpenters.

It was just as they'd known it would be. She came back from Carter's so pleased with herself that she'd been in a good mood for the rest of the day. She'd given Carter what for and told him he could get stuffed, she'd take her business elsewhere. She was all wound up, buzzing, like an engine running at full throttle. It was always like that, when she'd had a row. And if it was a row with outsiders, then it meant she'd let up back at home. She'd be all smiles. You could relax.

She did bangers and chips for supper and got ice-cream out of the freezer. Even Gran got the treatment – jokes and teasing till she dropped that stupid hangdog look she usually had and grinned and cackled a bit.

Later, their father cashed in and went out to the pub. He didn't often do that. Partly because she got ratty if he did, and partly because he wasn't that bothered anyway. He hadn't got any time for people, so he wouldn't talk to anyone, but he liked a beer.

She put the television news on – she wanted to get the weather forecast. On the screen there were people running, women dragging children, and then the noise of gunfire. The picture changed and you saw bodies lying in front of a shop. The boys looked at this bit with interest. Michael peered at the screen. You could see an ad outside the shop for Coke, just like you'd see outside the shop in the village, but the writing on another ad was in a foreign language and the shop had a funny name.

'See that?' he said. 'I dunno where that is but they have Coke, just the same as here.'

Their mother glanced at the screen. There was a dead person now, flies crawling on his face. 'Of course they do, stupid. Some things you get everywhere, all over the world.'

Michael thought about this. He wasn't really very interested, but her being in a good mood had made him feel like talking.

'But how do you know that? You haven't ever been anywhere. Anywhere outside England.'

She snapped the television off. She stood in front of him, her hands on her hips. 'Say that again.'

He'd blown it. He felt the familiar cold trickle in his insides. He knew that Peter had gone tense. 'I just said . . .' he began.

'You don't know anything, do you? You don't know anything about what I've done and where I've been, do you?'

He picked up the *North Somerset Herald* and pretended to be reading about the Young Farmers' Rally.

She walloped the newspaper so that the sheets flew out of his hands. 'I'm talking to you, Michael. I said what do you know about what I've done and where I've been? And you can wipe that look off your face, Peter. Is something funny?'

They stared at her. This moment melted into all the other times she'd exploded like this, like a crack of thunder, throwing you off your balance so all you could do was stare and wait for it to finish. She'd done that when they were two and three, and four and five. She'd done that before they could remember. It was the first thing they did remember – her face close to theirs, shouting.

'I've been to plenty of places you've never even heard of. I've been all over America.'

'Well, I didn't know that, did I?' Michael mumbled. 'You never told us.'

'I don't tell you everything, do I? I've driven all over America in a Cadillac car. Before you lot were born. Before I was saddled with you. I was six months on a ranch in California.'

'Well, they'd have Coke there, I suppose,' he muttered, too quiet for her to hear.

'Shut up,' she said. 'Just shut up.' She walked out into the kitchen.

They were both of them as big as she was now, but it never felt like that. When she turned on them they were still half her size; she reared above them and their stomachs ran cold. They stiffened in expectation of the clout that might come, the whiplash of her hand. She didn't clout them now, not any more, not for a long time, but the feel of it was still there, the anticipation, the shock when it came.

Once, they had had a Staffordshire bull terrier pup. Their mother had made a low plank fence to stop the pup getting into the yard where the rabbit pens were. When the pup got big it could have jumped over that fence easily, but it never did, because it thought it couldn't. They were like that dog.

Sometimes they knew that but couldn't say so, except in a certain way to each other. 'This is her, right?' they'd say, when they were knocking in a nail or chopping a log. 'This is one for her . . .' Wham! Smash!

After she'd gone out of the room they didn't even look at each other. Presently Peter turned the television on again. It was the weather forecast and she'd missed it.

When the television news was over Stella switched off and sat staring at the blank screen for a moment, chilled by what she had seen. She had been to a conference once in a city near the place in which these things were happening, had driven through that landscape, observed and talked to people doing daily, ordinary things – filling cars with petrol and selling fruit and vegetables and serving coffee. Taking children to school. Dead now, some of them, with flies on their faces. She got up and delved for an atlas in the as yet unpacked boxes of books.

She found the place that had been on the news. Names that she recognized sprang at her from the map. We went there, she thought, and there and there. Once I stood looking at wall-paintings in a church just there – or at least the person I then was did so. And now I am here, and some of those people are not anywhere at all. Possibly, back then, I walked past those very people so horribly seen just now.

She turned to the British Isles section. The west of England. There am I, she thought, just there alongside the thread of that road, at the foot of that brown range of high ground. And there is the pub where Dan and I stayed long ago.

When Stella contemplated her own progress through time and space, she saw lines – black lines that zig-zagged this way and that, netting the map of England, netting the globe, an arbitrary progress hither and thither. And sometimes these lines crossed one another. The intersections must surely be points of significance – these places to which she had been twice, three times, many times, but as different incarnations of herself, different Stellas ignorant of the significance of this site – that she would revisit it as someone else. But this progress of hers took place on two different planes. The web was not flat but of three or indeed four dimensions – it had to incorporate both time and space in the way that only physicists can imagine. Stella thought of those spiderwebs that form an airy complex density of minutely connected strands. Her space–time progress was something like that, the whole thing shimmering with these portentous nodes at which the future lay hidden. You walk blindly past the self that is to come, and cannot see her.

So, Stella, now. Standing in an unfamiliar house, an atlas in her hands – a tall spare woman, dressed in trousers and a sagging sweater, her hair a gingery profusion spiked with grey, perfunctorily twisted into a knot at the nape of her neck and skewed with a plastic clip. Narrow feet, long limbs, thin, elegant fingers that turn the pages of the book. Her face is thin, too – long pointed nose, wide mouth, blue eyes with a fold of skin dipping down now above and a web of wrinkles below. Never a conventionally beautiful face, you would decide, but arresting. You might glance, then look again.

Chapter Three

Michael said, 'Did she go to America before we were born? Was she on a ranch in California?'

Ted Hiscox swung his head round from the innards of a tractor. 'She said that?'

'Yeah.'

Their father dived into the engine again. 'Maybe she did. If that's what she says. Get me a can of oil.'

They had not always lived here at the bungalow. The boys knew that because both carried in their heads murky images of an elsewhere, a number of elsewheres. They did not compare these images, perhaps because it did not occur to them and also because it was as though that time had never been. There was a door slammed shut. 'What d'you mean?' she'd say. 'Where were we before we came here? We were somewhere else, weren't we, stupid? What's it got to do with you, anyway?' Their father was much the same. 'I dunno when we came here. Ten years ago, something like that. What's it matter?'

These patchy visions of other places were in any case dominated always by her presence. They were just the blurred background to her hectic action. She was having a row with their father, or bawling them out for something they'd done. Sometimes there were other people involved. Once she had had a dust-up with a man in a car-park who'd taken the space she wanted and when he'd gone she got a screwdriver and scraped lines on the man's car. Then she'd let them have a go at doing that and it had been brilliant. They'd done it since, several times, and both knew that the other remembered.

They both carried, too, the time she banged their heads together and then left them crying on a dusty pathway somewhere. Her hands grabbing them and the raging pain in the skull and each other's red ravaged face and her not there any more, just the dusty empty path.

So they had not always been here in Somerset. This fact did not particularly interest them, but they considered it from time to time. And every now and then, she would go on about things she'd done or things she knew about. Like the ranch in California. But then if you talked of that again, she'd lash out, like as not, and say you were talking nonsense. They'd start wondering then if she'd said it or she hadn't. She could get them so they weren't certain any more if she'd said something or if they'd imagined her saying it, like they were confused sometimes between things she'd done and things they knew she might do, was capable of doing.

You never knew where you were with her. She flew from mood to mood. And in good moods she said things that no longer held at other times. Or else she'd never said it. Like the business about agricultural college, last week. Michael had asked her about it.

'When am I going, then?'

'Going where?'

'To that college.'

She was sorting through a pile of bills in the place she called her office. She didn't look up. 'You're mad. What are you talking about?'

'You said I'd got this scholarship.'

'You haven't got any scholarship. When did you take any exam?'

He stood there. She went back to the bills. 'Get out of my hair and go and help your father. I don't know what you're talking about.'

He could hear her voice in his head, telling the woman in the shop in Kingston Florey: 'Michael's got one of the scholarships to the agricultural college, one of the top scholarships – we're going to have to learn to do without him.' In a loud voice, so people looked round at her.

'You said it in the shop, this morning.'

She turned. 'You're mad. I didn't say that. D'you think you're being clever or something? Why would I say something like that?'

And then he wasn't sure any more. He told Peter: 'You were there too. You heard her. Didn't she say that – about the college?' And he saw in Peter's face that he was uncertain now, too. She had always been able to do that – get them so that they didn't know what had happened and what hadn't happened. She'd tell them they were lying till they supposed they must be.

Their father wouldn't help. Never. He'd either back off or clam up, like with the ranch in California. 'If that's what she says . . .' They hung about while he fixed the engine and then he drove off and they went to their place in the hedge and banged around with sheets of corrugated iron. They were making a shed. They'd been making it for a long time, mainly because they liked the feeling of swiping away at the metal.

They were going back to the house when the new woman from Vine Cottage turned in from the lane and came walking down the path towards the mineral line. When she got to the track leading to their dad's work sheds she stopped and stood staring across at the big tractor. They went to pass her, not looking at her, but she started talking.

'Which of you was it I saw going past yesterday? Tell me something – are all tractors either Massey-Fergusons or Fordsons?'

Grinning away at them. Silly old cow. The way she talked got up your nose.

'Is it true they come kitted out with stereos and central heating these days?'

Still grinning. Thought she was being funny. They swerved past, left her standing there. Staring at the tractor. A Fordson, but they weren't going to say.

She had been thinking about tractors in Orkney. In Orkney they have the oldest tractors in existence. Pared-down rusting frames, nothing but an engine and a seat and a steering wheel and two great tyres. She used to notice the names when she was working on the island – flowing letters of chrome pinned to the radiator. Massey-Ferguson and Fordson and something else. What was the something else? She had noted them at the time as though the prevalent makes of tractor were also data of some kind, to be filed away along with the complexities of relationship between Fletts and Scarths and Rendells. She stood in piercing winds talking to men with leather faces who sat on their battered hulks of tractors and mildly answered her queries about their grandparents because they were amiable people and you didn't get a lot of visitors on the island. She was a change from the archaeologists and the bird people, they told her. And yes, my grandfather married a Flett, but my father's father, now he married an incomer, a Shetland girl . . . They'd sit on their Massey-Ferguson or their Fordson and the wind blew the pages of her notepad and the sea birds rode above her head calling. Oh, social anthropology is a joyous thing, she had thought, summering among these kindly folk, burrowing in their rich ancestral compost. In her roaring forties she'd been then, her head boiling with ideas and enough energy to walk off the horizon.

The tractor upon which she now gazed bore little resemblance to those old crates driven by Orcadian farmers in the seventies. This was a shiny scarlet affair, its cab high off the ground and screened behind perspex windows, its dashboard a marvel of dials and levers. What is that central lever for? she wondered. It occurred to her that this must be the state-of-the-art development of a gear stick she remembered on the Orkney bangers. What was that third trade name? She needed suddenly to know. And so when she caught sight of the two boys she called out to them: 'Tell me something – are all tractors either Massey-Fergusons or Fordsons?' She smiled encouragingly. They were sullen-looking boys with crops of dark hair that hadn't been washed recently enough and a hunched way of standing. Mired in adolescence, poor lads, she thought. She'd been sprayed with muddy water yesterday, as the tractor roared past without slowing down, but never mind.

No answer. Forging ahead, determinedly avoiding her eye. Not a forthcoming pair, it would seem. She tried again. They walked away, silent.

No joy there, she thought, mildly put out. She had always got on well enough with the young. She glanced after the boys. In order to reach the mineral line, you had to leave the lane some way beyond the cottages and the Morgan farm and strike off across a field which gave access also to the Hiscox business. A sleazy place, the bungalow and work sheds stuck in the middle of a shaggy area rife with nettles and thistles. A rough track led from the lane across the field to the group of buildings alongside which were ramshackle wire enclosures and wooden hutches. On another occasion, she had glimpsed ducks huddled in one pen, another heaving with rabbits. There were bits and pieces of machinery scattered around, a great pile of rusting metal and corrugated iron, another of old tyres. A couple of carcasses of spent cars. A decayed combine apparently sinking into the ground. Muddy puddles, oil spills. The bungalow was shabby – a stucco job, put up presumably before the time of such refinements as planning permission. A concrete path running up to the front door, the garden a perfunctory affair of unmown grass and some leggy shrubs.

Mrs Hiscox was a small skinny woman with blonde hair tied back in a pony-tail. She had stopped her car in the lane a few days after Stella moved into the cottage.

'Finding your way around?'

'I am indeed. I haven't walked so much for years.'

'I'm Karen Hiscox. Our place is along the lane – you'll have seen. Well, walking's not something I've got time for myself. Family round my neck and a business to run.' She seemed a person charged with some kind of manic energy; her foot continued to rev the car engine as she talked.

'I'm the idle retired,' said Stella.

'Plenty of you round here. Well . . . have to get on . . . give those louts of boys their dinner. By the way, if you want rabbit for a casserole, or fresh duck, you know where to come.'

'I'll bear it in mind,' said Stella to an already moving car.

Conversational exchange in these parts was most usually carried out between open car windows, Stella had learned, or from window to walker. She now knew by sight and by name the other inhabitants of this small hamlet, but had rarely seen inside anyone else's home. The Hiscox business was at the end of the lane furthest from her own cottage – in between were three other cottages and a farmhouse. Her nearest neighbours were an elderly couple whose stumpy home of cob and thatch seemed to act as a bulwark to prevent its steeply pitched back garden from cascading down into the road. Old Mr Layton could be seen there, day in and day out, fossicking among his rows of vegetables, while through the front window his wife was visible sitting peaceably in front of the blue glow of the television. Both were born and bred a mile from here, Stella had been told. Their daughter lived in Kingston Florey but their son – well, their son had moved away. Moved right away. To Bridgwater – all of fifteen miles.

In nice contrast, the neighbouring cottage was inhabited by weekenders – a family from Bristol. Dormant through the week, the place erupted on Friday evenings as the loaded Renault Espace arrived. Whooping children, the smack of a football, whiffs of interesting cuisine. Later, the windows would flare and the garden floodlights snap on. The parents were Tony and Linda, both IT consultants and loudly amiable. They plied Stella with local information – the best pubs, the sources for organic vegetables. They declared themselves absolutely fascinated by her former occupation and wanted to be given a run-down of a field trip. Egypt they knew well – they'd been on a cruise up the Nile to Luxor. She must come round and tell them how it was for her. But when she accepted an invitation to Sunday brunch the occasion was so corroded by fractious children and the problems of a sulky barbecue that her tentative account of the Delta back then was rapidly quenched. The relationship was diminishing to one of determined bonhomie whenever they passed in the lane.

The Morgans were the sole farmers. Genial enough but busy – and no wonder since John Morgan appeared to be cultivating much of the surrounding landscape single-handed, save for the considerable efforts of his wife Sue, who was never seen out of gum-boots, stumping resolutely around the barns. Such encounters as Stella had had with either were primed with the sense that some urgent task had been suspended and she would feel obliged to curtail the conversation.

There was also Stan, who lived in a cottage of such dilapidation that its walls seemed in danger of simply melting into the muddy pitch that passed for his garden. Stan was in business as an odd-job man, occasional hired labourer to John Morgan and purveyor of fuel. The yard behind his house was piled high with logs and sacks of Coalite. Stella had availed herself of this resource and was thus on greeting terms with Stan. They would exchange the mandatory comments on weather and temperature, but that was about as far as it went. Further intimacy was not encouraged.

That, it would seem, was local community life. As a connoisseur of such, she felt mildly disappointed. Oh well, she thought, it's no skin off my nose – I never was one who depended on a nice chat over the garden fence.

'Ah,' said Richard Faraday. 'Marks and Spencer's leek and bacon quiche. One of my favourites. You've discovered the Taunton shopping facilities, obviously.'

She had forgotten what a tall man he was. A long, lank

figure, his knees awkwardly bumping her too-low table. He had always towered over Nadine. Small, neat Nadine – dumpy in later life.

'If it's any help, I can let you have a list of local suppliers. There's a good baker in Williton.'

'Thank you – that would be very useful.'

A pause. The conversation kept withering. He had arrived on the dot, bearing a bottle of wine. A house-warming present. Not to be drunk now. Unless of course you want to. Personally I don't drink in the middle of the day.

'I am a member of the local chapter of the Council for the Preservation of Rural England. And the Exmoor Society and the local history group and that sort of thing. You may want to follow suit. It gives one a context. I can send you the addresses.'

'I'll think about it,' said Stella. 'I've never been much of a joiner.'

He wore a tweed jacket and grey flannels – the self-conscious leisure wear of a man who has worn a suit all his life. Poor old Richard. You spend forty years manipulating the economic life of the nation and then end up being the treasurer of the local history society. I bet he's the treasurer.

'Anyway . . . you're settling in all right?'

'Fine,' she assured him. 'Just fine.'

Or you cruise the globe, trying to find out why human beings do what they do, and then . . . Poor old Stella?

'Anything I can do to help – just give me a ring.'

'That's very kind – I will indeed.'

The shadow of Nadine hung there – the uneasy link between them. Something should be said. You must miss Nadine. I wish Nadine and I had seen more of each other. You must realize that Nadine and I hadn't really known each other at all well for over thirty years.

'We're entirely different types,' says Nadine. 'Probably just as well.'

She is talking of physical appearance. They are both in their underclothes, getting ready for a commemoration ball. This state of undress points up the distinction, it is true. Nadine is short and plump. She has a pointed cat-like face with notable green-gold eyes and the clear creamy skin that can go with very dark hair. Stella is long and leggy with an undulating pre-Raphaelite tawny-red mane and a permanent rash of freckles.

'Why just as well?' enquires Stella.

'We attract different types of men.'

'We're quite different in other ways. It's peculiar we get on so well.'

'That's why, silly,' said Nadine. She stands in front of the mirror, intent upon her eyes, which are being given the full treatment with mascara and eye-shadow. She waves the mascara brush at Stella. 'Do you want to try some?'

'No. It makes me look like a pierrot.'

They have arrived here from very different backgrounds, too, propelled on to the level playing field of higher education by brains and application. Stella is the late only child of unassertive parents who are still startled to find that their supposed ugly duckling is apparently a swan, in academic terms, and one of the chosen few. Her father, an accountant, has commuted to the same City office from the same suburban semi all his working life. He is beginning to be alarmed by Stella and will be entirely bewildered as time goes on. Her mother does some voluntary work in the Oxfam shop on the high street and otherwise devotes herself exclusively to scrupulous maintenance of the house and the servicing of the family. She is proud of Stella but becoming increasingly nervous of her. As the Oxford years go by she can find less and less to say to her, except to offer diffident advice about clothes and diet, which Stella smilingly ignores. Stella's eventual choice of occupation will throw them both into an unsettling state of respect, anxiety and dismay. When they both died in their early seventies, within a year of each other, Stella found that she had loved them more than she knew, but also felt released from some guilty obligation of perpetual reassurance.

Nadine is the youngest of a brood of five, the children of a showy barrister whose name crops up in newspaper accounts of big murder trials. 'So *embarrassing*,' says Nadine. Her mother is half-Spanish, which accounts for Nadine's eyes and colouring – an exuberant, cushiony woman who descends once a term, packaged in silks and furs, drifting Chanel No. 5 and shrieking with horror at the spartan college accommodation. Nadine is forever embroiled with her siblings; quarrels and reconciliations reverberate between Oxford and Richmond. Her older sisters arrive, dressed to kill, and sit fastidiously sipping Nescafé in Nadine's room while they tease her: 'Miss Education here.' Her brothers drive down in MGs and sweep the girls off to the Trout or the Bear at Woodstock, where Nadine flaunts them at anyone she knows. One of them takes a shine to Stella and is sharply warned off by Nadine: 'Don't you dare! She's much too clever for you and anyway she's *my* friend.' Stella and Nadine tell one another that they would like to swap families, but neither is sincere. 'Your parents are so sweet and *quiet*,' says Nadine. 'Honestly, the *peace* in your house.' Stella observes the Richmond household with amusement and the occasional twinge of envy, but knows that it is alien to her soul.

Stella considers other differences between them. Principally, Nadine is not much interested in her overt reason for being at university. She is only committed to her subject in so far as it is her guarantee. She is here for the fringe benefits of higher education, as indeed are many undergraduates. But she is intelligent, or she would not have got a place, she is energetic and she does enough work to get by.

Stella is frequently absorbed by what she has to read and write. She is simultaneously daunted and exhilarated – daunted by her perception of the range and profundity of knowledge and her recognition of the fact that she can never do more than scratch the surface, exhilarated because she has realized that learning is the arousal and satisfaction of curiosity. And she is abidingly curious. Sitting in libraries, she has come to see that for the rest of her life she will be prompted to ask questions and try to find answers. She feels as though her mind is expanding, month by month. Sometimes it seems to brim over with discovery.

She is fond of Nadine. She enjoys Nadine's company. They are a conspiracy, a gleeful, greedy alliance in pursuit of experience, of pleasure, of laughter, of whatever there is to be had through the accelerated passage of these three heady years. Each recognizes the distinctive flavour of the other and knows that they are not alike, but that, for the moment, they are caught up in the intimacy of being young and about the same business in the same place at the same time – an association as intense in its way as love or marriage, and one which quite eclipses later forms of friendship.

'OK,' says Nadine. 'Frocks on!'

They are both wearing strapless evening dresses. Nadine's is a froth of lilac tulle over a stiffened nylon petticoat, with a wide satin sash in a deeper shade. Stella is in plain dark green brocade taffeta. Both of them have their torsos clamped tight within rigidly boned bodices. Both wear elbow-length white nylon gloves which will be discarded and lost as the night warms up. Indeed, both dresses will be dreadfully abused. They will be peppered with small burns from cigarette ash, they will be splashed with wine. They will be creased and torn and grass-stained and Stella's will eventually be so saturated in muddy river water at the bottom of a punt that she will throw it away when she gets back to her college room at eleven the next morning. Track suits might be a more sensible uniform for the night ahead, but that would never do. Nadine and Stella are extravagantly parcelled for one of the major rituals of undergraduate life. Neither of them will lose their virginity tonight because both already have. Nadine will get bored with her escort and make a bid for someone else's, while Stella will overdo the champagne and end up asleep at dawn in that punt with a man she has never met before.

But at this moment they are untarnished. They inspect one another.

'Ravishing,' says Stella.

'Irresistible,' says Nadine.

They grin.

'And what decided you to settle in this part of the world?' said Richard.

He had told her about the several holidays he and Nadine spent around here. He had described his house and the search for it. A meticulous, methodical process, as one might expect.

She could have replied: you did, in a way. A provocative statement, strangled at birth. She bit back an alternative: I, too, have been here before. One would not want to have the matter pursued.

'Reasonable climate. Glorious landscape. As you said in your letter. I have friends in Bristol.'

And house prices are lower than in many parts. Though I note that your house was considerably more expensive than mine. Which is to be expected – civil servants are better paid than social anthropologists. A point appreciated by Nadine, who was into wage differentials long before I was.

'Lovely,' says Nadine, surveying the flat in Birmingham. She does not mean this, and the survey does not take long. A turn of the head suffices. There is a single room, with kitchen and bathroom slotted into windowless spaces more like cupboards than rooms.

Stella laughs. 'Come off it. You wouldn't be seen dead here.'

'At least it's nice and light.'

'It's what's called a studio flat. Euphemism for only one room.'

'You could do more with it,' Nadine decides briskly. 'You need some cushions to brighten it up. And a different lamp. I know a woman who'd make you new loose covers for the couch and the armchairs really cheaply.'

'I'll bear her in mind.'

'What are you *doing* here exactly?' Nadine's tone perfectly expresses her perplexity, concern and barely suppressed disapproval of what she perceives as her friend's present plight. 'Do you know, I've never even been to Birmingham before. I mean, it's a place you knew was there but not that you'd ever think of going to. At least not on purpose.'

Nadine and Richard are now living in Sevenoaks, in an old farmhouse with a big garden. This means rather a lot of commuting for Richard, but it is so much nicer for Lucy, who is now two, to grow up outside London.

'I teach. And when I get the chance, I talk to people on housing estates about their attitudes towards their parents and their grandparents and their uncles and aunts.'

Nadine registers this but is not sufficiently interested to wish to know more. 'What about social life?'

'Are you asking if I've got friends to go to the cinema with?' Nadine giggles.

'No,' says Stella. 'There's no man right now. At least none I'm encouraging. God, you don't change, Nadine.'

Stella and Nadine are still within reach of their former selves. They can still slip back for an instant into that climate of shared experience, the shorthand of mutual concerns. Very soon — a few more years — this community of spirit will be extinguished. They will be launched upon the divergence of direction that will take them into their different lives.

'What do they pay you?' asks Nadine.

Stella tells her.

Nadine is aghast. She stares at Stella in horror. 'Richard gets heaps more than that.'

'I don't doubt it,' says Stella.

'Richard knows what he'll be getting in five years' time.'

'Lucky old Richard. I don't even know if I'll have a job in five years' time.'

'Are you worried?' Nadine soberly inquires.

'Not particularly.' This was true, she was not. Something

would turn up. And in the event it did. 'I'm not a planner, like you. I bet you've already worked out which day to stop taking the pill so Lucy's sibling gets born at the convenient moment.'

'Sibling!' mocks Nadine. 'Listen to you, you've even started talking jargon. Actually,' she goes on complacently, with an instinctive glance down at her stomach. 'Since you mention it . . .'

'Congratulations,' says Stella. 'Aren't you clever! Oh – and Richard.' She tests herself for a twinge of envy, of resentment, and finds that there is none. Quite genuinely there is none. Does this mean that she is wanting a vital component because she is without genetic drive? And if so, does it matter?

Perhaps it is just that she would not want to be Nadine, hitched now to an inexorable process, subsumed into the lives of her husband, her children.

One day, maybe, thinks Stella. Not now. Not yet.

Richard was talking about the daughters. 'The girls are attentive, but of course they have their own agendas.'

Stella tried to remember what they did. She had seen them briefly at the funeral, women in their thirties valiantly greeting people through tears only just held back. 'Oh, Stella,' they said. 'Mummy was talking about you only last week.' Their eyes glistened. Richard was grim-faced. Stella could think of nothing appropriate to say. She mumbled conventional condolences and assumed that she would not see or hear of him again. She was surprised when she received a Christmas card and then another the following year in which he gave his change of address: ' . . . my retirement bolt-hole in west Somerset. You may remember that Nadine and I often used to holiday down here.'

Nadine had announced her cancer in a bleak little letter. 'I'm about to start some rather ghastly last-ditch treatment for a growth. Keep your fingers crossed for me.' When Stella visited her a few weeks later, she saw that Nadine was beyond the reach of either hi-tech medicine or superstitious encouragement. She was at home, a frail carcass beached on a sofa, her eyes dark pools in a white face. Richard clattered quietly in the kitchen, supplying refreshments at discreet intervals. The two women struggled to find anodyne matter for conversation. Stella felt the presence of their former selves, unquenchable in youth and fervour. She saw Nadine's twenty-year-old body, contained within a Kestos bra and a panti-girdle that was supposed to do something cosmetic for her hips. This image floated above the diminished, almost extinguished Nadine who lay there on the sofa. The real Nadine, the Nadine of then, sat in her undies in front of the hissing violet and orange columns of a gas fire, stretching out her fingers to dry the nail varnish, lecture notes strewn around her. But implicit within that moment was this one, Stella now saw, a dark inevitability lurking beyond them.

'Remember the fire escape?' said Nadine suddenly.

'I do indeed.' They looked through forty years and saw again the vertical iron ladder down which had shinned illicit male visitors to the undergraduate hostel.

'I had the fire escape room in my second year, didn't I?' Nadine continued. 'Very convenient, but it meant you had to put up with other people's men creeping past your bed in the small hours.'

'I went down it myself once,' said Stella. 'Just for the hell of it. You had to jump the last six feet. It's a wonder none of them broke an ankle.'

'Maybe they did and we never knew. Sports injury, they'd have had to say.' Nadine grinned, then flinched with pain. The smile faded. She stared bleakly at Stella. 'Well, long time no see, I've lost track of what you're doing. Still camping in mud villages?'

'No, I gave that up long ago. Professionally unfashionable nowadays, anyway. In fact I retire in a couple of years' time.'

'I suppose you do,' said Nadine. 'Like Richard. He's going to be on his own, I'm afraid, poor darling.' Her face suddenly crumpled. 'Oh, *shit* . . .'

And now Stella and Richard had moved from the quiche and salad to the choice of local cheeses ('Ah, you already know about the Stogumber dairy, I see'), and still Nadine hovered unmentioned. I know so little about her, thought Stella. She had realized this on that last visit: they had nothing in common except that time. The bond between them was the uneasy one of those who have been young together and then forge apart, but remain perversely united by those shared and heightened years. We are in each other's heads for ever, Stella had thought – not as we are now but as we were then. Nadine knows nothing at all about me any more and yet in some eerie way she does because once we were twenty.

Stella plunged. 'Did Nadine ever tell you about the summer vac when we hitch-hiked to the south of France?'

'Many times.'

Ah. Well, yes, I dare say she would, in nearly forty years of marriage. Stupid question. Even so . . .

'A well-worn theme,' said Richard, with a wintry smile. 'The lorry driver who bought you a bottle of red wine. Nude bathing in the Dordogne. Your version would be entirely different, I'm sure. Alternative evidence.'

'I wasn't proposing to give it. I was just thinking of her.'

'Quite so. As do I. Daily.' He wiped his mouth and folded his napkin. A chair leg faintly scraped.

'Coffee?'

'Thank you, no. I must be on my way.'

At the door he paused. 'Please keep in touch. Call on me for local information.'

'I will indeed.' He doesn't much care for me, thought Stella. Never did, I imagine. That could be mutual. And there is no reason why we should feel ourselves obliged to maintain an artificial association. A token exchange of civilities from time to time, that will surely do. He was helpful over finding the cottage and is dutifully welcoming, but no doubt sees me as a burden to be assumed for Nadine's sake. Which does not suit me – I who have never been anyone's burden.

She embarked on a brisk farewell. But he ignored her. He was silent for a moment and then said, 'Nadine thought the world of you. A sentiment I shared, if I may say so.'

Wrong-footed, she thought. How mistaken can you be? Or is this simply more of his unrelenting good manners? He thanked her for the lunch and departed abruptly. She gazed after him, vaguely puzzled, and saw his car elbowed aside by a green pick-up van which dashed down the lane from the main road.

Chapter Four

Their father was talking to a farmer who'd come about some combining he wanted done in August. Probably he wanted to give the combine a look over. People who came down about a contract could get angry when they found that half the things in the ad they didn't do. There'd never been a mole drainer and the bagging system was from when their father was in partnership with Everitt from Bishop's Lydeard. But she said, leave the ad the way it is, it looks better like that. So that was how it had been since for ever. And the combine was all right.

When their father had finished with this man, he was going to do a repair job near Carhampton. They'd decided earlier to get him to take them with him in the pick-up. Now they edged towards the door.

She waited till Peter's hand was on the latch. 'Where d'you think you're going?'

'Going with Dad on that Carhampton job. Give him a hand.'

'You're coming to Minehead with me. I'm taking Gran to the bank. You can go and pick up some stuff at the supermarket while I'm seeing to her.'

They'd been expecting that. She didn't like them going off with their father. She liked them where she knew what they were doing. She didn't want them away from the place, unless it was to go to school. You should know when you're well off, she said. There's plenty of mothers wouldn't give a damn. Turn their backs on their children and don't want to know. I'm not like that, and just you remember.

They were burning away at her, but there was no point in arguing. Anything you said she could say for longer and louder, on and on, for days if she put her mind to it. And their father wouldn't back them up, anyway. They might as well forget it.

It was every four weeks, the business of taking Gran to the bank. Their mother would have Gran's cheque book in her bag with the cheque written out and then Gran signed it in the bank, in her shaky writing, breathing hard while she did it, making sure of the name. And then the girl behind the counter gave her the money, a big wodge of it. Then they all went to the other bank, their mother's bank, and she paid the money into her account there. And after that she took Gran to the café for a pot of tea and a plate of pastries. That's what Gran had been waiting for, greedy old sod. She didn't make any fuss about going to the bank because she knew what came next. She'd sit there gobbling cakes, the crumbs dribbling down her chin. The boys hated that. They'd wait outside rather than have to watch, though they wouldn't have minded one of those cream éclairs.

It was always a performance, at the bank. Their mother laughed and joked with the girl behind the counter, or the man or whoever it was. They all knew Gran and asked her how she was and that, and Gran would grin and look pleased and their mother would do the talking for her, saying she was fine, aren't you, Mum? Or that she'd had a bit of a bad chest but was pulling round all right. Once, Michael asked her why she didn't just take Gran's money out of the hole in the wall, or take it all out instead of bit by bit when she needed it. She'd snapped at him not to ask stupid questions.

Another time, she'd said that one day Gran would have to go into the old people's home. 'Be better for her there. They've got professionals to look after them, and I can't be running after her for ever.'

Michael and Peter thought it would be better to send her there now. She was disgusting, Gran, in their opinion. She farted. And it turned you up watching her eat. But when one of them said as much, once, his mother flared up. 'You can just shut up. I don't want to hear that sort of talk. This is her home. She's my mother, isn't she? So just you pack it in, talking like that.' Only the day before, they'd heard her shouting at Gran about how she couldn't expect to have people dancing attendance on her and she was an ungrateful old woman.

Actually she didn't do much dancing. Nobody did. Gran just sat in her chair most of the time, like a heap of old rags, and to tell the truth she didn't really bother them that much. Most of the time they never noticed her. And she'd always been there.

When Gran's money ran out, she'd put her in the old people's home, that must be it. Fair enough.

Gran had lived in a big house once. She had a bunch of old photos in her bag, creased to bits, and one of them showed this big house with her standing in front of it, only young-looking and with a little girl who was their mother. Gran had dropped it on the floor once and Michael picked it up and they both looked at it. They weren't interested but it had been a bit surprising – that house, and Gran and their mother all different.

Sometimes she was quite nice to Gran. She'd tease her a bit and make jokes and Gran would cackle that old woman's laugh that was really irritating. But then next day she'd be shouting at her and Gran would sit huddled up like a dog that thinks you're going to hit it. Gran was sixpence in the shilling, she didn't know if it was Monday or Tuesday, sometimes she didn't even know her own name, but she watched their mother all the time, to see what might be going to happen – like people watch the weather forecast because there's fuck all you can do about it but you may as well know. They did the same themselves. In that way, it was the same for Gran as it was for them. It annoyed them, knowing that.

'Don't even think about it,' she said, making them jump. They'd been watching their father put tools into the back of the pick-up. The farmer from Taunton had gone. 'You're not going with him. Stop standing there like a pair of dummies. Tell Gran to get a move on.'

It was half-term week. It was only at half-term and in the holidays that they got lumbered with going to Minehead with her. On school days they were safe from that.

West Somerset Social Services – Health Visitor's Report:
Case No. 4670/921. Mrs Millicent Danbury

Mrs Danbury is eighty-six years old and suffers from Alzheimer's. She is resident with her daughter and son-in-law and is cared for by her daughter, Mrs Karen Hiscox. Mrs Hiscox is evidently much attached to her mother and shows her affection and attention. She is determined that the old lady should not be institutionalized until absolutely necessary, although she makes it clear that the present situation places a considerable burden on her. The home conditions are reasonable, although

43

somewhat untidy. Mrs Hiscox runs a smallholding in conjunction with her husband's agricultural hire and repair business. There are fourteen- and fifteen-year-old sons with whom Mrs Hiscox also appears to be much concerned.

This old lady is living in satisfactory circumstances in a happy family unit. Information was given about Day Centre facilities but Mrs Hiscox felt that her mother would become confused and anxious if removed at all from the home environment.

School was no problem. They had it sewn up. If anyone thumped either of them, they both of them thumped back, only harder. They stuck together as much as they could and people had learned to steer clear of them, not to try anything on. They didn't have any friends, but that was all right. And she'd said not to get mixed up with the other kids. 'They're rubbish, that lot,' she said. 'You keep to yourselves. And don't let any of them put anything over you.' She told them what to do if anyone did.

Letter from Mr George Tomlinson, Chairman of the Board of Governors of the Grove School, to Mr Daniel Chivers, Headmaster

Dear Headmaster,

I am writing in connection with a letter I have received from Mrs Hiscox. Mrs Hiscox complains that Mr Rogers of Form Four used verbal and physical violence in reprimanding her son Peter for a misdemeanour. The exact nature of the misdemeanour is unclear – Mrs Hiscox mentions a difference of opinion with another boy – but she states that Mr Rogers, in intervening and cautioning Peter, called him 'a stupid little git', slapped him about the head and in so doing bruised his face. Her elder son Michael was apparently a witness of the incident and bears out this account.

I understand from Mrs Hiscox that she has already approached you about this incident but is dissatisfied with your response. I am therefore obliged to investigate the matter and would ask if you and Mr Rogers could be available to discuss it with me at a time to be arranged.

Yours sincerely,

George Tomlinson

Letter from Mr George Tomlinson to Mr Daniel Chivers

Dear Headmaster,

I have received a further letter from Mrs Hiscox of which a copy is enclosed. I need make no comment, I think.

I recall the point you made during our discussion to the effect that the mother has expressed her intention of removing both boys from the school as soon as they reach the school leaving age. Since they are now fourteen and fifteen, it is merely a question of endurance, so far as you and the rest of the staff are concerned. I note that both boys are low achievers in academic terms and lack motivation. It is clear from the files made available to me that these boys have been an ongoing problem. Of particular note is the contradictory and extravagant nature of the complaints and allegations made at fairly regular intervals by the mother. May I convey my recognition and appreciation of the restraint that has been displayed by you and other members of staff in connection with this family.

Yours sincerely,

George Tomlinson

The boys knew that the teachers didn't like them and they didn't give a damn. They hated the teachers, anyway. They were a lot of stupid gits – and Michael had told one of them that once, when the teacher was hustling him. Besides, if any teacher picked on them, they only had to tell her and she'd be down there bawling them out, or shouting down the phone at them, or writing letters to the headmaster and people. And the teachers didn't care for that. Some of them were scared of her – Michael and Peter had seen it in their eyes when they stood behind her and she was on at whoever it was she'd come down to see, yelling at the top of her voice and saying the sort of things people like that don't get said to them.

So there wasn't anything anyone at school could do to them, in the end. They only had to tell her, and back each other up.

If she was on your side, you were fine. Not if she wasn't. They knew about that too.

Today she wasn't bothering much with them. It wasn't them she was interested in, right now. She'd been having a go at their father, the night before. She was still lit up. That was why she hadn't wanted them to go off in the pick-up, partly. She didn't want them and Dad getting together. Not that that was likely. Dad didn't talk much at the best of times. After a row he didn't talk at all.

He wasn't like her. When he was angry he went all quiet and that was worse, in a way. You waited for him to blow up, like a radiator. You waited for the bang and the hissing steam. But he was quiet most of the time, that was normal too. He said what had to be said and that was all. He never smiled. Hardly ever. She'd throw that at him when they were having a row.

'Po-face!' she'd say. 'You and your bloody po-face. Look, let's teach you how to smile. See?' And she'd stand in front of him with a great glaring grin, all her teeth bared. 'Like this,' she'd say. 'Got it? Smiling, this is called.'

Their father would slam out of the house, then. That was how their rows ended, usually – him slamming out and coming back hours later, reeking of beer probably, saying nothing to no one. And her as pleased as punch, singing about the place.

The boys weren't bothered. You were in the clear so long as you kept well out of it and didn't let her catch you listening or watching. If that happened, you'd be for it. The same went for Gran if she was fool enough not to pretend to be asleep or play even more batty than usual. But she'd learned to keep her head down. Maybe she wasn't so daft. There were times when you wondered – when you saw a look in her eye that made you think she was plain miserable and that was all that was wrong with her. Well, you would be, wouldn't you, if you were old like that? The boys told each other that old people should just be put away, like animals, in their opinion. That made sense, didn't it? You wouldn't keep an old dog hanging around, would you?

Their father had the pick-up ready now and roared off without a word. Their mother bundled Gran into the car. She shouted, 'Hurry up, you lot,' without turning round. They'd been behind the sheds, in the hope she might forget about them. Fat chance. She always knew exactly where they were, without looking.

She drove like she always drove, sprinting when she could, nosing up the back of slow cars, swerving out to overtake. That could be quite good fun – people's shocked faces as you went past and the driver's hand on the horn when she was already practically out of sight round the next bend. Or the flaring headlights in front as she cut in and the buzz you got, wondering if they'd brake in time, if she'd make it. But she always did.

She'd been had up a few times. Endorsements. But she hardly ever hit anything, just the odd near-miss. She was known for her driving. They'd heard her tell people she'd done racing driving when she was younger, that she had some sort of racing driver certificate. Or that she'd done driving for films, been a stunt woman. When they asked their father about that, he just shrugged.

But she was an ace driver, no question. That was the thing about her, she always had to be on top, to have the edge over the other bugger.

They'd be on the road, as soon as Michael was seventeen. They'd been driving the tractors for years, both of them, up and down the track. They'd drive the combine sometimes, too. They wouldn't need any lessons. Just for Michael to pass the test and they'd be away. Get an old banger and off.

Sometimes they talked about this. It was Peter who had the ideas – what sort of car they'd get and how they'd beef it up – and Michael who said, 'Yeah! Yeah – that's right, that's what we can do!' It was usually like that. Peter thought of something and Michael joined in and then they did it together. Or just talked, in the case of this car. Winding each other up – we'll get a Golf GTI . . . no, a Honda.

When they got to Minehead she parked the car and made for the bank. They were to go to the supermarket for some stuff and then meet her at the café. They saw her head off down the street – that swaggering walk, full steam ahead so people had to get out of her way, stopping at the zebra, impatient, to look back for Gran shuffling along behind. As soon as she was out of sight they went into Woolworth's for an ice-cream.

There were boys from school there, a whole bunch of them. Nudging and muttering. Not that they gave a shit. All those people at school were rubbish, like she said.

They met up at the Pick 'n' Mix. 'Going to the fair?'

So there was a fair, was there? Shooting galleries. The boys thought of this.

Now they were sniggering, that lot from school. Whispering. Got to get back to their mum – that's what they'd be saying. Fuck them. Fuck the lot of them.

They could beat them at shooting any day, given the chance. They were good at shooting. They'd shot pigeons with their father. Shot them dead and seen them fall.

'We're going down there now.' Grinning fit to bust, beginning to move off.

'Suit yourself,' Michael said. 'We're not bothered.' He nodded at Peter and they made for the video display and stood there as though they were trying to decide what to get. When they looked round the others were gone.

But they were pissed off now, thinking of the fair, thinking of that stupid lot from school. Then Peter said, 'We could do one now.'

'We got to get back to meet her.'

'We can do it quick.'

They had to buy a lighter because they'd not brought one. Then they went down to the front and had a look round. At one end there was no one about. They weren't longer than a few minutes. It was an easy job.

They were a bit later than she'd said they were to be when they got to the café and she let them have it, of course.

'Where've you been? What do you think you've been doing? D'you think I've got nothing better to do than sit around waiting for you?' And they'd left out two of the things on the list for the supermarket.

But they didn't care by now. They didn't care about her slagging them off so half the town could hear. They didn't care about those other boys or the stupid bloody fair.

She said, 'And what are you so pleased with yourselves about, I'd like to know?'

In the car she said it again. 'I'm talking to you, Michael. I'm asking you a question. And you, Peter.'

They looked out of the window, mouths slammed shut. They were at the roundabout now, on the outskirts of the town, in a knot of traffic. A police car whooped past, going the other way. Somewhere, they could hear a fire engine. They were cock-a-hoop, riding high. Stuff them, that lot from school. Stuff her, too. She thought she knew everything. Well, she didn't, did she?

Chapter Five

Dogs are to be found in the *Yellow Pages*, like everything else, Stella had discovered. The Animal Rescue Centre was at the end of a long winding lane, tucked into a hillside, and announced itself with a cacophony of barking which advanced and receded behind the hedgebanks as she drove onwards and upwards.

The place was run by a Miss Clapp, a huge woman in overalls, herself faintly dog-like – some stolid dependable St Bernard perhaps. She interviewed Stella in a room overflowing with sacks, tins of dog food and rusty filing cabinets, which seemed to double as office and food store. She said, 'There are several possibilities. Dog or bitch?'

'I hadn't thought.'

They advanced along the line of wire pens in which dogs either raced up and down or stood with nose pressed to the mesh. There were uncomfortable overtones of some prison compound or refugee encampment.

'You won't want her,' said Miss Clapp briskly. They were passing a German shepherd, sprawled asleep on the concrete. 'Came from a Chinese take-away in Bristol. Shut all her life in a back yard ten feet by six, poor beast.'

'What for?'

Miss Clapp rolled her eyes. 'Don't ask.' After a moment she added, 'Well, they're said to eat puppies, aren't they?'

At the next enclosure she halted. 'There's this,' she said doubtfully. 'But I shouldn't think he'd do, really.'

The dog in question was hurling itself at the wire and bouncing off. The creature was so engulfed in dirty greyish fur that you could barely tell which end was which – an animated bath mat sprang to mind.

'What breed is it?' asked Stella.

Miss Clapp shrugged. 'A cross. There's some old English sheepdog somewhere, hence the coat.'

She moved on. They passed two more enclosures, both containing animals that seemed to have been assembled from miscellaneous spare parts – a plumey tail erupted from a sleek low-slung chassis, a hound-like creature flaunted the curly coat of a poodle. It struck Stella that this was like the windows of a department store at sale time – marked-down goods from discontinued lines in styles and colours that had been a designer mistake in the first place. She paused before a small terrier-like creature that gazed imploringly.

'What about this one?'

'I wouldn't,' said Miss Clapp. 'She's in pup. Though I suppose you could have her spayed and abort all in one go.'

An appallingly high-handed way in which to start a relation-ship, thought Stella. I think not. 'What kind is she?'

Miss Clapp inspected the dog. 'Looks like Jack Russell and toy poodle to me. Not a cross that would have sprung to mind, I must say. But this chap next door might be a possibility.' She stopped again. 'He's more or less a springer spaniel. Something else has got in at some point – the legs are wrong – but you could say he's springer all but.'

Stella considered the dog. Not too large. Not too shaggy a coat. Posture expectant but amenable. Like the cottage, he seemed to fit the bill in all the basic essentials, so why look further?

'He's from a broken home,' said Miss Clapp. 'His mummy and daddy got divorced.' Catching Stella's startled look, she added, 'The previous owners. Both moving into flats and couldn't keep him – terribly cut up about it. I said, look, he's a sweetie, he'll walk out of here, you see. I've only had him ten days. D'you want to look him over?'

She undid the door of the pen. The dog emerged with a sidling movement as though to make himself as unobtrusive as possible, unable to believe his luck. He squirmed around their legs. When Stella bent to pat him he pressed himself to the ground in a convulsion of humility, like an acolyte in the presence of some priestly figure.

'Of course, they're anybody's – springers,' said Miss Clapp. 'Not the dog if you've been used to something that's entirely owner-oriented.'

'I've never had a dog before.'

Miss Clapp looked at Stella in astonishment. 'Oh, I see. Well, in that case I should think a spaniel – spaniel-type – would make as good a starter as any.'

Her previous relationships with animals had been transitory ones. There had been a little white cat in Greece, who arrived uninvited to share with her the room over the coffee shop. In Orkney a collie from the farm had elected to accompany her on her rounds. This bestowal of trust by another species was a startling gratification, she had noted. How can it thus assume that I will not abuse it, that I am kindly and well disposed? One felt charmed and chosen.

There are and have been few societies in which the concept

of a pet is unknown. But the cult of intense communion with a dog or a cat is that of Western affluence. New Guinea tribes are entirely indulgent towards the pigs which roam free and root around their villages. But the pigs are currency and indicators of status. The Hindu sacred cow enjoys a form of protection which would mystify the RSPCA. The hen in the kitchen of an Orkney farmhouse was not there out of sentiment but expediency. The curious elevation of domestic animals to quasi-human status is peculiar to certain societies and unknown in other places.

An atavistic instinct told Stella to give dogs a wide berth. A dog may be rabid. In the Middle East, in the Far East, in Greece and Turkey, over much of the world – she automatically moved aside from any dog or cat. In Egypt, in the Delta village in 1964, there was always a stone or two in her pocket to keep away the pye-dogs.

Extract from the diary of Stella Brentwood, February 1964. Quarto-size ruled exercise book. Green cover with black lettering: CAHIER. Some pages stained. The cover faded and with further stains.

I don't understand why the pye-dogs are tolerated. To a considerable extent they are not, of course. They are driven off and maltreated. The children torment puppies – no one interferes. The pye-dogs are not fed, but allowed to scavenge. So what are they for? When I ask, people shrug. They are there, said Dina – uninterested.

Questions, questions. All day long I ask questions. I put down question and answer in the field-diary, which is as dry and detached as these things are supposed to be.

This is a different kind of diary. One in which I try to answer questions myself.

How can I get a glimmering of how these people see the world? How can I shed all my own assumptions, beliefs, prejudices, etc., and get some murky intimation of what goes on in Dina's mind as she sits there outside the house door making fuel for the fire out of dung and straw?

One possibility is to go back in time. This is not to say that Dina is a chronological freak, that she is stuck in a time-warp, that she is historically retarded. None of that. Simply that one way for me to understand how she sees the world is through my knowledge of other societies within time as well as within space. I am an agnostic. Dina is deeply religious. I am a sceptic. Dina believes in ghosts. She also believes that her donkey sickened and died because of the malevolent thoughts of a neighbour. She believes that she must shield her baby from my glance because my blue eyes might do it harm (though she would concede that this would be quite inadvertent on my part – I am a perfectly decent person, it is simply that I have blue eyes, which is unfortunate). The baby wears a string of blue beads which help to avert the evil eye, it seems. I am puzzled by the logic of this. Why blue, if it is blue which is suspect in the first place? And when a pedlar came through the village hawking similar beads, Dina advised that I should invest in some myself, which I have duly done. Best not to reason why. But is she suggesting this as a precaution against self-inflicted injury, or malevolence from elsewhere?

If I look at these beliefs within a different context I see that they would be entirely familiar and reasonable to – say – a resident of rural France or England in the seventeenth century. Dina's system for dealing with the irrationality of fate would be instantly recognizable. The ghastly things that happen cannot be arbitrary – someone or something must be manipulating events. God ordains, and has to be appeased. Spirits, neighbours and the devil conspire to do evil but can be foiled if you know the right recipe. Dina has called in another neighbour, known to have powers of sorcery, who will do some stuff with various potions and incantations that will put paid to the donkey-slaying neighbour. And she would no more dream of passing up her daily prayers, or her observance of Ramadan, than she would cease to eat, drink and care for her family.

I am not treated as one of the family but as a combination of honoured guest, gullible customer and wayward child. I rent a room in this house – the home of Saleh and Dina and their offspring – which is one of the more substantial village houses. By my standards the house is a mud hut topped with a stack of straw and invaded from time to time by poultry and goats. By theirs, it is the enviable and appropriately superior abode of one of the village's leading families.

I am mildly unwell a good deal of the time and distinctly ill on occasions, despite stringent precautions. The family watch with fascination and amusement my daily water-boiling ritual. They are equally intrigued by my medicine box, though they would not wish to avail themselves of its contents. Dina looks upon my quinine tablets and antibiotics with just the same scepticism as I view her sorcerer neighbour's pills and potions.

I am covered in mosquito bites. I have had three boils, a bout of impetigo, a septic foot, flu, bronchitis – and diarrhoea more times than I like to recall. I am also continuously stimulated, invigorated and excited. Everything about these people is either illuminating or mysterious or both.

I am a problem to Dina's husband, Saleh, as indeed I am to everyone in the village. I am not married, which is patently a personal disaster, attributable either to catastrophic lack of charm or some other more sinister factor such as proven ill-temper or perhaps some hereditary ailment (these speculations have been passed on to me, of course, with apparent innocence

– in fact inviting either confirmation or denial). It is difficult for the men of the village to rate my sexual appeal (or lack of it) since I am so far removed from any recognizable benchmark – tall, fair, the physical opposite of their own women. So I become a kind of neuter so far as they are concerned, but since I am technically female, this question of my non-marriage remains baffling. The women are especially sorrowful on my behalf. They shake their heads in regret – at thirty-two what hope is there for me? Some of them are grandmothers at that age.

The expectation of life in the Nile Delta is not much above forty.

The villagers are curious about my private life – or rather about my apparent absence of private life – but they are surprisingly incurious about my role amongst them. They seem to accept without query my intense interest in their lineage structures and give equable though incomprehensible answers to my barrage of questions about the number of their cousins and their relations with their maternal uncle. Of course, family is a favourite subject the world over. Here am I, willing and indeed eager to listen for hours on end to a breakdown of emotions, affiliations and resentments which is no doubt as therapeutic for them as it is rewarding for me.

Everyone in this community is related to everyone else, pretty well. There are three main families, though the dividing lines are blurred by inter-marriage. So in a community of around two hundred, all are known to each other and anyone over the age of ten would have a pretty clear idea in their head of who stood in what relationship to whom. The place is ruled by blood and genes. Everything that anyone does is deter- mined by his or her position within this complex network with its inflexible set of obligations and taboos.

Certain people may walk unannounced into Saleh's house.

Others may not cross the threshold under any circumstances, on grounds of social inferiority or some ongoing feud. The class system flourishes, even within what is in effect an extended family. Some are more equal than others in the village. One of the most conspicuously unequal, a half-blind elderly widow, is Saleh's uncle's wife's cousin, but this connection does not inhibit Saleh, Dina and everyone else in the household from treating this neighbour with lofty contempt. 'She is a very poor sort of person,' explains Saleh. 'She is not important. There is no need for you to talk to her, ya sitt.' Saleh considers that he has a duty to monitor my researches.

Trachoma, the eye complaint that frequently leads to blindness, is endemic in the Delta. In the village there are eighteen blind adults, a further group who are partially blind, and a whole raft of children who exhibit disturbing signs of incipient disease.

Dina's third child, a two-year-old boy, has a dubious-looking eye. Dina has it in mind to take him to the eye clinic which comes once a month to the large village five miles away, of which ours is a sort of satellite. So far a convenient opportunity has not arisen – either Dina is too busy when the day comes, or the lorry which serves as a bus service between the villages is full up. In the meantime Dina is having Yussuf's eye treated by the neighbour with the line in sorcery who attended to the matter of the donkey. This man's treatment is known to be highly effective, she explains – probably just as good as the clinic and with the advantage that you know what you're getting, no nonsense about new-fangled pills and creams that you don't understand, let alone those needles in the arm.

Yes, I have made my opinion known. There is a point when professional detachment becomes inhuman. Strictly speaking, I should be here simply as a pair of eyes, a pair of ears, an interpretive mind. But I am stuck with the tiresome human tendency towards emotional response. And in any case all social anthropologists meddle. They meddle by the very fact of their presence. Better to meddle constructively when the opportunity offers.

Dina heard me out tolerantly. Maybe next month. If the cotton is harvested. If the sweet potatoes are planted. If there is room in the lorry.

My other frailty, in the eyes of the village, apart from my lack of a husband, is my poor Arabic. I improve, both in speech and comprehension, but I am still woefully deficient. This is hilarious to anyone under eighteen and a matter of faint solicitude to everyone else. Few people here have come across a foreigner at close quarters before. Some of the older generation remember the war years, when the Delta ran with foreign troops, but none of the army bases were nearby and there was little or no personal exchange. So I am their first experience of an otherwise normal adult who cannot talk properly. They correct me – kindly or impatiently according to temperament. And of course this crippling inadequacy has an ambivalent effect upon their perception of me – I am an educated person (though a woman), a doctor – but I talk like a child. They know well enough that I have my own language in which I am presumably competent, but all they hear is this fractured Arabic. They know who and what I am, but they cannot help feeling that I am also – well, a bit simple.

And within the context of this place, that is perfectly true. I am a simpleton, an ignoramus. Almost every subtlety of social exchange is lost upon me. Saleh and his family, who feel responsible for me, have to tell me how to behave correctly, as you would a child. They have to tell me how to address whom, how to come and go, what should or should not be said. My many expensive years of education have left me quite unequipped for life in this mud village with two transistor radios, one moped, one petrol-driven engine and two hundred people, many of whom cannot write their names. What it has given me is the urge and the ability to cast a cold eye upon them and their way of life.

Do I find this uncomfortable? Of course.

Yesterday I took my notebook out into the fields, which offers good opportunities for one-to-one interviews, if you can find someone taking a rest from field-work, or watering animals, or just sitting down for a gossip. Nobody labours flat-out in these parts. That is one great advantage of the revolution – with the overseers gone and their land to some extent their own, the fellahin can adjust to their natural pace, which is slow.

Ibrahim and his son Ali were comfortably installed in the shade of the fig tree by the water wheel, while their gamoose clumped round and round, blindfolded and harnessed to the wheel. There is something deeply soothing about the creak and groan of the wooden water wheels.

'Sa'ida, ya sitt,' said Ibrahim.

'Sa'ida, ya Ibrahim,' said I.

Greetings completed, I sat down beside them. I am never able to squat as the fellahin do – there seems to be some anatomical difficulty – and have to sit with legs outstretched or leaning upon one elbow like someone at a picnic. Naturally enough, this is thought eccentric and amusing.

Some preliminary chat. Then, with Ibrahim's consent, I embarked on routine kinship questions. Ali, a cheeky fourteen-year-old, interrupted with embellishments and elaborations, mostly libellous. His father slapped him down half-heartedly.

'In your country, ya sitt,' said Ali, 'who are the people who ask many things and write in notebooks?'

An unsettling question. An illuminating question, further-more. Ali is on to something. Ali has looked over my shoulder and beyond my notebook and perceived that this set-up has implications. His question nicely nails the problem.

Everyone in the village is aware of the reason for my presence, that I have no official status and that co-operation with my enquiries is entirely voluntary. In the event, virtually everyone has volunteered – to be left out is seen as social annihilation.

And now here is Ali with his beady fourteen-year-old eye upon the matter.

I try to explain. I say that such questioning does indeed go on in my country and that I myself could be one of the questioners. But all this stretches my Arabic to its utmost and beyond. Not surprisingly, both Ali and his father lose interest. I give up and seize the opportunity offered by a pair of pye-dogs who are lurking just beyond our oasis of shade. I put the pye-dog question. Why are they tolerated? Do they serve some purpose?

Reminded, Ali lobs a stone at the dogs. Unlike me, he aims to hit. The foremost dog departs, squealing.

'They are created by Allah,' says Ibrahim, nicely begging the question.

Occasionally Stella comes across this battered testament among her papers. If she glances into it she views its author with benign curiosity – this is herself, it would seem, but a self she finds it hard to recognize. Some of the experience cited she remembers; she reads of the rest with faint surprise. The place itself surges back, conjured up by those handwritten pages: the smell of dust and dung, the sound of carts and donkey hoofs and crowing cocks and raised voices, the blinding sun. She rather approves of this young woman who was reflecting so keenly upon the problems of being an anthropologist, but is bemused by other sections. The exchange in the fields is entirely unfamiliar. Did this really happen thus? The narrative detachment gives the episode a fictional flavour. When did I write this? she wonders. The same day? Or weeks later, grooming the raw material into this considered anecdote? And for whom was that young woman writing? Well, for this *alter ego*, as it turns out, in the quirky way of diarists. And if the pye-dog query is apocryphal or manicured, there is no question but that a lifelong ambivalence towards dogs stems from those months in the Delta.

This dog, then – this almost-spaniel – would serve to tame Stella. He would extinguish finally her atavistic dog-stoning inclinations. He would confer respectability and give her a conversational entry with those she met on her local walks.

How things would be between them became clear within the first few days.

Stella liked the dog. She found him vaguely companionable, the touch of his silky fur against her leg or hand was pleasant. But the dog did not like Stella – he adored her, he worshipped her, she was the pivot of his existence. Thrust into a position of unwilling exploitation, she felt an irritable guilt. There was an appalling imbalance of feeling. It was like associations in the past with men who had fallen for her but for whom she could feel nothing more positive than a mild affection. The dog watched her every move with liquid, fearful eyes lest she might be proposing to go out and leave him. Each time she approached the front door he would scrabble imploringly at her knees. If she did go out without him, she could hear his desperate howling as she got into the car, and when she returned he greeted her with an enthusiasm of welcome and forgiveness that left him too breathless to bark. Each time she passed him in the cottage he wagged his tail in propitiation. When she patted him he collapsed in ecstasy. Did all dog-owners spend their time subjected to this relentless emotional pressure, she wondered?

'I'm not sure that this is working,' she told him sternly, at the end of the first week. But by then there was no going back.

Chapter Six

'If you've had your fill of writing articles, try something more punchy,' says Judith. 'A memoir. Do a *fin-de-siècle* Malinowski.'

Stella pulls a face.

'No material?' This is guile.

'Oh, I've got diaries and stuff like that stacked up somewhere. Photos, even. Cuttings . . .' Stella's voice trails away.

'I didn't mean that sort of material. I meant, surely it was interesting enough.' The guile now is transparent.

'Of course it was interesting,' says Stella hotly. 'Good grief, one hasn't spent half one's life pigging it in disagreeable climates for no good reason.'

Judith smiles complacently.

'Oh, *you*,' says Stella. 'Winding me up . . . All right, yes, I suppose I could write a memoir. But I haven't the slightest inclination. And that's not false modesty, either.'

Judith shrugs. 'Suit yourself.'

'Come to that, what about you?'

For Judith too has served her time in disagreeable climates. She is an archaeologist. When Stella first set eyes on her, she was squatting in a trench somewhere in Malta, so caked in dust and sweat as to be apparently wearing camouflage. She had squinted up into the sun from under the brim of a grubby bush hat and told Stella kindly to push off, they weren't taking on any more labour. Thus began an abiding friendship.

'No way,' says Judith. 'Though I grant you that I may be in need of occupation. I have it in mind to cash in on the tourism boom in these parts – up-market archaeological tours. A kind of West Country Swan Hellenic, in a luxury minibus. Trouble is, where do I get the cash for the minibus?'

Judith and Stella have dropped in and out of each other's lives according to circumstance for the last thirty years. Their friendship is elastic. It has withstood long periods when they have not set eyes on one another, and weathered also spontaneous holidays with shared rooms in spartan hotels.

Judith Cromer lives in Bristol with her partner Mary Binns. She has sporadic work with an archaeology unit, work which may well run out due to shortage of funds. Archaeology is not a growth area these days, tourism or no tourism. Mary Binns is better placed, as a radio producer. Stella is not all that keen on Mary Binns, who has green eyes and is convinced that there is something going on between Stella and Judith, which is far from the truth and ever has been.

Years ago Judith said to Stella, 'Have you honestly never ever fancied another woman? Not even a *frisson*?'

Stella reflected, trawling through a lifetime of sexual responses of varying degrees of fervour, and had eventually been able to come up only with the head girl at school on whose account she had felt weak at the knees for the whole of one term. 'What about you and men?' she retaliated. To which Judith replied that she tried one once and never again, thank you very much.

Mary Binns is mistaken, but to this day she hovers suspiciously on the outskirts of the friendship, greeting Stella with exaggerated warmth when they meet, treating Judith to pained silences when she has been with Stella. Judith makes light of this and says simply that Mary has her difficult side, don't we all? She sounds like the archetypal spouse stoically making allowances, and Stella is sometimes surprised that it is Judith and not she who has ended up in a state of tetchy domesticity. Judith is not the homely type. She is restless, maverick and enquiring. What she likes best is to be scratching in the dirt with a trowel somewhere hot and ancient. But here she is, now in her mid-fifties, living with Mary Binns in a flat in Bristol, doing the occasional hurried survey when excavations for a new motorway or hypermarket turn up inconvenient material of archaeological interest.

'Grounded,' says Judith suddenly. 'I suppose that could be said of both of us. And one should resist. Your dog seems to have some problem with its foot.'

They are heading back to Stella's cottage after a walk along the wide grassy track which marks the course of the old railway line that once carried iron ore from the mines on the hills down to the coast. The mineral line. This physical relic of a forgotten industry cuts through the fields and becomes on the flanks of the hills a thickly wooded track which climbs to the ruins of the old winding-sheds. The mineral line can be reached on foot from Stella's cottage by following a bridlepath leading from the field beside the Hiscox place. It is a good place to exercise the dog.

But the dog, today, is behaving like a recalcitrant child. Too far, he is apparently saying. Too hot. Now he is limping. He plods reproachfully at Stella's heels. 'He comes from a broken home,' she explains to Judith in extenuation. 'He's used to a suburban back garden.'

'I can't think what's come over you,' says Judith. 'You avoid commitments for forty years and then land yourself with this.'

'He confers respectability. Everyone has a dog in these parts.'

'Most people in inner cities have dogs, as far as I can see. Preferably the kind that are just a set of fangs on legs. At least this creature isn't that.'

They have left the mineral line and are now crossing the field. The dog has perked up, home within reach, and veers off in skittish pursuit of a pigeon. The Hiscox boys come rattling in off the lane on their bikes, narrowly missing him as he runs across the track. One of them yells, 'Sod off!'

'Hmm . . .' says Judith. 'Is this local form?'

'By no means. These lads are just disaffected adolescents, I take it.'

'What we've been spared . . . Do you ever wish you'd had children?'

'No. You?'

'Well, no. Does this make us freaks? And truth to tell, I get on a storm with the young. But I'd rather they were someone else's.'

'My sentiments entirely. But it's aberrant behaviour. Distinctly freakish. The norm is to stake out your claim in the kinship network, establish your credentials by way of offspring. Get yourself into the gene pool.'

'Not at all,' says Judith. 'It's simply a system to ensure a controllable labour supply. Children are useful disposable goods – barter their services for essential commodities, if the opportunity offers, stick them out on a hillside at birth if needs must.'

'Extreme behaviour,' objects Stella. 'The product of complete social breakdown.'

'Not at all. Common practices in antiquity.'

And thus, by the time they reach the cottage, the Hiscox boys are quite forgotten, subsumed into one of those pleasurable arguments that have always been a feature of their friendship.

'The trouble with us,' says Judith over a lunch of bread and cheese, 'is that our trades have put us out of touch with the real world. The one we have to live in. I think in terms of funeral practices, weaponry and ubiquitous bloodshed, and you see people as components of kinship networks and lineage patterns.'

'That sounds precisely like the world as I know it. I only have to switch on the telly or read a newspaper.'

'Oh, well, the royal family are doing you proud.' Judith laughs. 'And global violence is nicely up to standard. Point taken.'

'But you're right in another sense. We don't conform to social expectations. Unmarried, no children. We're the sort that would have been burned as witches, in other times and places.'

'Or consulted as oracles,' says Judith. 'You have to pick your moment, if you're inclined to nonconformity. As it is, I'd say we don't do too badly.'

The phone rings. It is Mary Binns, who greets Stella effusively and says that she just needs a quick word with Judith, if it isn't too much of a nuisance. Judith, returning to the table after a brief exchange, looks sheepish and explains that Mary wants her to pick up some groceries on the way back. It is silently understood that the issue is that of the establishment of possession, not a stop-off at Tesco.

'You'd better not leave it too late,' says Stella. 'Or you'll hit the rush hour.'

'Huh . . .' says Judith. 'Trying to get rid of me, are you?'

Back in the Malta days there had been someone called Rosie – a nut-brown girl as wiry, fiery and maverick as Judith, so that she seemed some kind of providential clone. Stella, herself emotionally preoccupied, had enjoyed their company and felt a benign empathy. But Rosie had vanished and now there was Mary Binns, and Stella would not presume to ask how Mary Binns had come about. Or what had happened to Rosie. But in her mind's eye she sometimes sees Rosie and Judith, sprawled in the shade of an olive tree, drinking red wine – vibrant, sun-baked, light-years from today and a Bristol branch of Tesco.

Judith gathers herself to leave. 'Well,' she says, 'I can see you're nicely dug in. Incidentally, I'm still not quite clear why you plumped for here rather than anywhere else.'

Stella hesitates. 'Happenstance, I suppose. Richard Faraday sent me stuff from an estate agent – you remember Nadine, my old college chum? And I came this way once with Dan.'

'Pure fluke,' says Judith. 'So it goes. That's how we all live. Now for a bout with Tesco . . . See you soon.'

But when she has gone Stella looks again – back to that olive grove of the sixties – and sees that it is not so at all. She sees that time as inextricably entwined with this one. They are both woven into a tapestry, united by an inevitable thread of circumstance. There is a fourth figure present on the day of the olive-tree picnic, he who will subsequently say, 'Anywhere . . . so long as it's somewhere rural and blindingly English.' The roof under which she now lives was already hinted at then, along with the line of hills at which she looks, along with the metamorphosis of herself. Not happenstance, she thinks, not happenstance at all, but the way that the future is implicit within the present, did one but know. The signals are already there but we cannot read them.

Stella was finding that she lived now on two planes. There were all the familiar references of her own past and present, tapped into daily by way of visitors such as Judith, by letters and phone calls. But there was also this new backcloth, this social and physical landscape of which she was now an element. She eyed it with interest, and saw that she in turn was watched.

She talked, she walked, she drove. She looked and she listened. She did what she had always done in pursuit of her work and would now be incapable of not doing – she noted everything she saw or heard, and the place began slowly to take on a further dimension. The invisible swam into sight, like the hidden shapes in a child's magic drawing book.

First she learned her way around. She visited Minehead and Dunster and Williton and Watchet. She learned the structure of the place, its systems of linkage and dependence. She saw what people were doing now and she dipped into the ubiquitous past, proffered in the form of brochures and pamphlets and murky postcards, to discover what they used to do. She wandered around villages, read the names on the war memorials, leafed through the local papers and saw the same names. She pottered in churchyards. She followed footpaths around the edges of the fields, along mysterious sunken tracks or over bracken-covered hillsides. She drove down lanes that became green tunnels between the high hedgebanks. She pored over the map, which served up names that could have furnished some pastiche of a perished countryside: Dumbledeer, Felon's Oak, Sticklepath. And wherever she went, whenever she could, she fell into conversation – sometimes with people she would never see again, sometimes with those who became a circle of acquaintance.

A couple in a pub at Watchet told her that they'd thought it would be more like Ilfracombe, and these narrow roads were a menace. A potter in an Exmoor village (every village had its craftsperson, she soon realized) had fetched up there after spells in Crete and Provence and thought the light was amazing, but had to avert her eyes every time the hunt passed by.

The postman told her much. The postman bore a Welsh name – his forebears had probably crossed the Bristol Channel to work in the iron mines up on the Brendon Hills. He told Stella who was married to whose sister and which farmer's daughter worked at the NatWest in Williton and why the agreeable cottage on the edge of the village was falling into decay (an executors' dispute over ownership). He defined the neighbourhood. He told her who was a bona fide product of this place and who was not. She saw herself defined as he spoke.

And thus Stella learned. There came beams of light. The place took shape. It ceased to be a landscape, a backdrop, and became an organism. Stella perceived the intricate system of checks and balances by which things worked. She saw that there was a continuous state of negotiation, of dealing, of to-and-fro arrangements. Everyone stood in a particular relationship to everyone else, often literally so in terms of marriage connections or distant ties of blood. People employed one another, or sold things to each other, or exchanged services, or simply rubbed shoulders here, there and everywhere. Each casual encounter in a lane or at a shop entrance reinforced this subtle and elaborate system, as hard to penetrate as any she had met.

For there were two layers here, she saw. There was the basic and significant layer, which went back a long way – two, three or more generations. These were the people whose parents and grandparents looked out from here and who continued to do so themselves, for whom these parts were the hub of things and elsewhere was . . . elsewhere. Though, admittedly, a rather more familiar elsewhere nowadays, thanks to several decades of mass communications and package holidays. But grafted on to this layer was a further one, the layer of subsequent settlement – some of it transitory, some more permanent. Most transitory of all were the summer visitors – a valuable source of revenue for some, a confounded nuisance for others. Then there were the more abiding settlers – the retired, the owners of holiday cottages, the potters and the woodcarvers and the weavers. These were digested, up to a point and depending upon their personal achievements in terms of participation and commitment. But they would never be truly attuned. They would never be able to plug into the elaborate communication system which hinged upon intimate knowledge of how things stood, how things had changed and why, and what this implied in terms of expedient response and reaction. They would always tramp around wearing blinkers. They would always speak with a foreign accent.

Stella moved warily amid these intricate connections. People were willingly communicative. It is not entirely true that the English are a grudging lot, mean with their favours. If the approach is considered sufficiently harmless or even congenial, there is no stopping them. And a woman in late middle age is the most neutral figure of all, Stella discovered. She poses no sexual threat nor challenge. For young men, she is of so little interest as to be effectively invisible. For women younger than herself, she is a comforting reminder that they have not themselves got that far yet, thanks be. For those around her own age, she is a reassurance: we are not alone. Accordingly all three groups are reasonably well disposed, the defences are down, an overture will be accepted with equanimity and in some quarters with enthusiasm.

Stella realized that she had been too young, back then. She had been too young out there in the field, as anthropology so bizarrely calls the baffling world at which it stares, introducing overtones of botanical study. She had been too young in the Delta and in Malta and Greece and even Orkney. She had been still a viable woman, with all that that implies. As soon as she stepped into view, the waters were muddied by the implications of age and gender. Both men and women wondered how it was possible for her to be doing this. Men might wonder if she was available, or alternatively if she was to be taken seriously. Women did not know whether to pity her or to envy her. It was not feasible for her to be perceived with neutrality. Her foreign status was one thing, her age and gender were another and equally to be taken into consideration.

Now that it was too late, she found herself with this protective camouflage. West Somerset would cheerfully bare its soul to her. She had only to get talking at a bus stop or supermarket check-out, share a table in a pub, stop to chat at a filling station. Her credentials were instantly apparent: agreeably spoken, no spring chicken, origins uncertain but that's what you expect these days. Nothing to be lost in a passing exchange (though probably nothing to be gained either).

It was too late, in terms of her trade. She had not the slightest desire to set about some neat little study of kin groups and systems of integration in a rural community. But in another sense it was not too late at all. This new persona was thrust upon her – like most people she felt ambushed by time – but since it had to be, there were certain advantages, she saw. The old and the young are washed to the margins of life – unessential and dependent. They share only the opportunity for untrammelled observation. And for Stella observation had been her way of life.

Certainly, the wider landscape offered more rewarding scope for both observing and sampling some kind of community life than the small enclave of the hamlet along the lane, where she had little to do with her neighbours. The old couple next door occasionally emerged as far as the gate, in which case a few words were had. The farmer would bestow a perfunctory grin and wave from his tractor. Karen Hiscox would wind down the window of her car to hand out some piece of advice – 'If you need your vehicle seen to, don't go to that place on the crossroads, they'll do you down' – or indulge in a fleeting assault on the pleasures of family life: ' . . . with boys, and especially with boys of that age, you make it clear who's boss and no nonsense, if you know what's good for you – that's me, and frankly my husband doesn't want to know, off on a job as soon as there's a problem.' The weekenders would call energetic greetings if they saw her in the course of one of their noisy, child-encumbered walks.

It was a far cry from her professional experience. She remembered the dawn to dusk interactions of the Delta village, of Greece, of Malta. The old men sitting on a bench under a tree. The street corners on which there was forever a knot of talking women. The informal conference centre that was the shop or the coffee house. The comments and interrogations shouted from doorways. The small excursions on foot from here to there for no particular purpose other than to see who might be around. The house to house visits in pursuit of information or for the exchange of commodities or to pass on some succulent piece of news. In other words, the fervent face to face community life of a world largely innocent of cars and telephones, for better or for worse. What have we come to? thought Stella.

At the same time, she noted the ambiguity – the downright hypocrisy perhaps – of her own response. Would she wish to live like that herself? Is she, indeed, attempting to live like that now that the opportunity is offered? Well, no. She, too, retreats behind her closed door and into the protective shell of her car, from which a wave and a smile will suffice. Her professional life has been that of a voyeur, her interest in community has been clinical. She has wanted to know how and why people get along with each other, or fail to do so, rather than sample the arrangement herself. She has been simultaneously fascinated and repelled. Moving around the world, she was always alert, always curious, but comfortable also in the knowledge that, in the last resort, this was nothing to do with her. Indeed, casting a cold eye back, it now seems to her that she and her like can be seen as parasites. Intellectual parasites.

But she was after something more than observation. She was no longer in the business. Now was the time to prove herself. Even if she could not hope to melt into the ancient levels of this place, even if the immediate community of the lane was a touch unpromising, there were still slots into which she could fit in the wider context. Join things, she told herself sternly. As advocated by Richard. Participate. You are still carrying around a mental notepad and pen – trash them. Join the human race. After all, it is your subject.

Chapter Seven

'But it would be neither local nor history,' Stella protested.

Richard Faraday sighed. 'Ten meetings a year. We have already wrung dry the possibilities of the Brendon Hill iron mines, the pre-history of Exmoor, the Bristol Channel shipping trade . . . The net gets thrown wide, by necessity. Last year we had someone's cruise on the waterways of Russia, with accompanying video, and an account of plant-collecting in the Himalayas by a retired curator from Kew. Both warmly received. You would be a star turn. Please, Stella.'

'Oh, well . . .' she said. Then, 'Are you the treasurer?'

'I've recently been elected secretary. The dogsbody role. Hence my plea.'

'All right. If I must. "Lineage structures in the Nile Delta" or "Neighbourhood and community in a Maltese village"?'

'I think . . .' Richard hesitated. 'If you could frame it rather more as a . . . perhaps a sort of travelogue. Would this feel like professional degradation?'

'By no means,' said Stella. 'I shall look on it as a challenge.'

The local history society met in the village hall, a small wooden building perched at the edge of a recreation ground. Chairs had been arranged in a group at one end of the room, near to the table with the tea urn, an attempt to domesticate a space which seemed to invite gym displays or flower shows rather than discussion.

'Don't be daunted by the size of the audience,' said Richard Faraday, greeting Stella at the door. 'Fifteen is par for the course. These are the hard-core members, the enthusiasts. I'll introduce you all round before we start.'

Identities swam forward. The sprightly woman in her fifties farmed on the Quantocks. The silver-haired man in a blazer who was helpfully adept at setting up Stella's slide equipment was a retired teacher. That familiar face was the lady who ran the plant nursery in a nearby village. The young couple were potters from the craft centre ten miles away. The two teenagers so valiantly attending were doing A-level history. They would have to put this occasion down to experience, poor dears, thought Stella.

She had decided to talk to them about the baffling nature of cultural identity, basing the discussion around the proposal that interpretation is distorted by expectations. To this end, she had brought along a selection of slides which would illustrate her point, provide diversion and serve as the required travelogue. Once the group was settled, with cups of tea in hand, and the projector proved to be functioning properly, she gave a short introduction. The social anthropologist, she told them, studies human societies in order to understand more about how we behave by recording the range of differences in social behaviour and organization. But the anthropologist, like anyone else, is governed by his or her own beliefs and expectations, and has to learn how to sidestep these for penetration of the codes of the society under study. She treated them to a few illustrative anecdotes from her own experience, explaining that her specialism was lineage patterns and kinship structures. 'There is plenty of existing material on this for comparative studies, but I never wanted to be a desk anthropologist – I always wanted to get out there into the thick of it.' People's expressions went from that of polite neutrality to something warmer. They glimpsed Stella as someone younger, more exotic and more provocative, who had lived in a mud hut in Egypt and there made social gaffes, who had had to come to terms with misogyny, religious fervour and a sweep of prejudices and superstitions. Not to mention polluted water supplies, rampant insect life, problematic food and climatic extremes. She saw herself regarded with increasing interest.

'Right,' Stella said. 'Let's have the first slide.' The blazered teacher went into action. A brilliant square of tropical landscape sprang on to the screen, luxuriant growth amid which foraged a number of small pigs, observed by a tribesman wearing a loincloth. 'Now what do you see here?'

Reflective rustling from the audience. Then the Quantock farming lady waded in. 'Well . . . some sort of cross, I'd say. There's a Tamworth look to them, but the boar's much too lightly built. They're like something from a rare breeds place. Not much meat on them.'

'Is that sugar-cane they're eating?'

'What's that gorgeous red flower?'

'Surely the point is the chap,' said the teacher. 'Aren't we meant to be thinking about him? What's the stick-thing he's holding?'

'Stella,' said Richard Faraday, with edgy restraint. 'Do please enlighten us.'

Stella explained that the pigs were indeed the focus of interest, and that these were indeed pigs, pigs somewhere in New Guinea, though she was afraid that she could not specify the breed. But these pigs were significant far beyond appearances. They were meat, and would indeed end up consumed, but to the New Guinea tribesman, they represented a form of wealth more crucial than mere food. The pigs represented a system of political checks and balances on the trotter, as it were. The pig herd would be built up over a period of years and, in due course, slaughtered at an extended ceremony of feasting and dancing which would serve to establish the strength of neighbouring groups and set up future alliances in tribal warfare. To their owners, the pigs are not mere pigs but the means to a further round of aggression and territorial expansion.

'A new twist to the concept of the arms race,' said Richard.

There were questions about how the pigs were cooked, about tribal numbers, about weaponry. If her presentation was to be kept on track, Stella saw that she would have to curtail the discussion and forge ahead.

'Were you there yourself? I mean, did you take the photo?'

Stella replied that she herself had never worked in New Guinea but that the pig culture is a famous instance of complex and initially puzzling social behaviour and for that reason she had wished to use it as an example. 'And now we'd better move on to the next slide . . .'

The pigs were replaced by a display of shell ornaments – bracelets made from a single curved slice of shell with some fibre fronds hanging from it, long strings of small pink shell discs with shell pendants and further shell strings attached. Once again, she asked the audience what they saw.

The responses were now more cautious. 'Jewellery,' someone ventured. 'Primitive jewellery? Sort of local craft things – that they'd sell to tourists?'

'Actually, no,' said Stella. 'What you see is not for personal ornamentation at all. These pieces are never worn. They are the physical manifestation of a complex system of political and economic relationships. Shells – yes. The armbands are made from trochus shells – the necklaces are strings of pink spondylus shell discs. Quite pretty, to our eye, but worthless. To the Trobriand islanders, however, they are each entirely distinctive, of inestimable value and loaded with implications.' She went on to describe the Trobriand ceremonial exchange system called Kula, whereby such objects are passed around between island clans in a byzantine process of receipt and obligation, the function of which is variously interpreted as the confirmation of political hierarchies or the safeguarding of trade relationships by way of an established network.

'The EEC springs to mind,' said Richard Faraday thought-fully. 'Or, to go further back, the Hanseatic League. A long-established concept. Very shrewd of them.'

'They must be the devil to thread, those tiny shells,' said the lady from the newsagent. 'Would they have needles?'

Stella allowed the comment and discussion to continue until it once more showed signs of getting out of hand and then called for the next slide. 'New Guinea again – a most instructive place, New Guinea, anthropologically speaking. Now what do you think all this is about?'

They were now looking at a log-constructed building, the entrance to which was hung with shield-shaped objects brightly painted in black, ochre, red and white, with what might be stylized human features – grotesque eyes and mouths set amid swirling lines and patterns. In front stood a group of tribesmen, naked except for feather head-dresses, shell and feather necklaces, and curved yellow protuberances attached to their penises. These phallic adornments were so long and unwieldy that the ends had to be supported by lengths of twine attached to the shell necklaces.

Stella's audience considered this slide with caution. They were all conditioned by long exposure to television documentaries and knew that such sights are not a matter for ill-bred and ill-informed derision or merriment. At least most of them did. There were one or two pockets of resistance which became apparent when Stella said, 'Any comments?'

'Not in front of the ladies, I'd say.' This came from a bluff middle-aged man who had made little contribution hitherto but was now chortling with appreciation.

The woman from the plant nursery said, 'To be quite honest, those shield things with faces look like what you see pinned up on the classroom wall in the primary school.'

Stella stepped in. 'The phallic décor is much as you might expect – a statement of virility. A threat, possibly, to rival tribal groups. The shield-like objects at the hut entrance are tamburans and represent the ancestors. They are respectful references to the abiding power of the tribe's ancestral past. They remind the tribesmen of their mortality and set them within the context of time. They are icons consecrated to the collective memory.'

'Is that how they think about it?' enquired the Quantock farming lady.

'Good question,' said Stella. 'No. It's how I – we – think about it. We interpret their perception in terms of our own.'

This statement had a rather silencing effect on the group. Stella decided to produce her trump card.

The screen now showed an aerial view of a row of suburban

semi-detached houses, several with satellite dishes and three with garden gnomes on the front lawn.

The audience stared. There was some laughter.

'Acacia Drive, Surbiton,' said the potter from the craft centre. 'I know it well.'

'Look at it with an alien eye,' said Stella. 'What is there that is puzzling?'

Someone proposed the satellite dishes. 'Personally I don't think Sky is worth the candle. Nothing but sport and bad films.'

'May I have a shot?' said Richard. 'I suppose that if I were a visiting Trobriander – or Bushman or Inuit or . . .'

The woman from the plant nursery interrupted. 'Those are Eskimos and they'd have Sky. I know because there was a programme on the Arctic, about how they're losing their traditional skills, and you saw the concrete bungalows they live in now, all with TV aerials and dishes.'

Richard waited with strained courtesy until she had finished. 'Or anyone with an untutored eye, I'd say that what we have here is a culture given to the display of totemic objects related to a form of sun worship.'

This idea caught on. It was pointed out that the gnomes, too, could be religious ' . . . like Catholics having Christ on the cross in their living-room' (a rustle of protest here – this was perhaps a bit near the knuckle for some).

'Quite,' said Stella briskly. 'Anyway, you take the point – interpretation is through the eye of the beholder, with all the inevitable accompanying distortions. We see only what we already understand.'

She had struck just the right note, Richard assured her as

they sat down for dinner later. Informative without being patronizing, stimulating without being impenetrable. 'You went down very well. I shall bask in reflected glory.'

She had already noted the menu with disapproval. She did not like pricey restaurants. Not that she didn't enjoy a quality meal from time to time, but a bill the size of someone else's weekly income was offensive. This part of the evening had prompted her strongest reservations. 'You must let me take you out for a meal after as a due reward. I insist.'

So there they were, amid the soft lighting and pale pink napery of some establishment with all the airs and graces induced by frequent Sunday newspaper coverage.

'I don't come here often,' said Richard. 'Only when a decent excuse appears. So . . . what have they got today? Their fish items are usually pretty good. The scallops are probably worth going for. Snails I've always drawn the line at, I must say.' He shot a glance at Stella. 'Which will seem very wimpish to you, I dare say. You must have eaten a fair gastronomic range, in the course of duty. It is *de rigueur* to adopt the local diet?'

'It can be expedient. Often there's nothing else. I've not been exposed to the more esoteric menus. The Australian aboriginal repertoire . . . Grubs can take some getting used to, I'm told. They twitch. Sorry . . . don't let me put you off. All this sounds delicious.'

And a terrible waste of money, she thought, but never mind. His privilege, if he so wishes. And I have always been rather too ascetic in my tastes. Which is just as well, or I could never have done what I've done or been where I've been. But it's congenital, I suspect. I was ever thus. Couldn't be bothered much about clothes and prinking, either. Not like Nadine. Great prinker and clothes connoisseur, Nadine.

And Nadine swims into vision, towing Stella round Elliston & Cavell, hoicking garments off rails, hustling her into changing cubicles. 'You've got to have it, you look amazing in it.' 'But I don't need it. Anyway, I can't afford it.' 'Well, I think you're mad not to,' says Nadine. 'But of course you look amazing anyway, blast you, when you want to. It's always the people who try least . . . it's not fair.'

Looking up, Stella caught sight of Richard Faraday in the wall mirror, suffused in flattering strawberry-gold light – the well-preserved older man, one would think, like a tanned actor in some commercial for insurance policies – and with him this woman, thin-faced, coppery hair flecked with grey, who is also given some subtle cosmetic treatment and appears for an instant like an elegant stranger with some haunting familiar echo.

If you have been a beauty, ageing must be intolerable, Stella thought. The process is bad enough as it is – the ebbing away of possibilities, the awful tyranny of the body – but for those who lose their very trade mark, it is savage. No wonder so many elderly actresses take to the bottle. I should count myself lucky, who have never set much store by my own face.

'So how are things going?' said Richard.

She was taken aback for a moment. 'I'm sorry?'

'Acclimatization.'

'Oh, that . . .' Concentrate, she told herself. The man is not a mind-reader. And he is paying for your dinner. 'Fine. I know my way around. I have a dog, for better or for worse. Time does not hang heavy, so far – by no means. I say – you were right about the scallops. Perfect. The sauce tastes faintly scented.'

Richard smiled complacently. And I sound gushing, thought

Stella. Uncharacteristic behaviour induced by this place, which is not really my cup of tea. And I still have to get through the fricassee of chicken breasts, chorizo, peas and thyme, not to mention an operatic selection of puddings.

'Food is always more than meets the eye, of course.'

'You mean there's no such thing as a free lunch?' said Richard. 'This dinner is quite without strings, I assure you.'

'No, no – I mean that it usually has ritual significance, the world over. Restaurants not least. The McDonald's ritual is quite different from the ritual of a place like this.'

'Well, so I should hope. Not that I've set foot in a McDonald's since the girls grew up. So what is the hidden agenda here?'

'Reassurance,' said Stella. 'The customer is being told that he is indeed in the depths of the countryside but, never fear, the resources of civilization are available. Mud and muck there may be, but immunity is available for those with discrimination.' And a credit card, she was about to add, and then remembered that she was a guest.

'Hmn.' Richard eyed her. 'I suppose that's one way of looking at it. Another could be that the customer is flattered by special effects – ' he waved a hand at the swagged chintz curtains, the beamed ceiling, the displays of lustreware – 'and grandiose cuisine. He feels that this sort of thing is his natural due and decides to come again.'

'Does it have that effect on you?'

'No, but I'm a hard-headed civil servant, impervious to corruption. I simply come because it's the best place within twenty miles for a good meal. I bring the daughters here when they visit.'

'I hope that's often,' said Stella, feeling that she had perhaps been rather too combative a companion. 'I mean, I hope they're able to visit you a lot.'

'They're busy, but they come when they can. And I retaliate, of course. Laura is in London now . . .' There was a fragmentary pause and then he started to talk rather deliberately about an exhibition at the county arts centre. Stella realized that he had felt himself to be treading on dangerous ground, in the presence of one who was childless.

'Nadine always knew she wanted children,' she said. 'That surprised me, when we were young – that she could be so sure. She knew even when she was twenty. By the time I was thirty, I knew for certain that I didn't.'

He was relieved that he had not been tactless, she saw, but with the relief came a cool look. He found this declaration unnatural, or unwomanly, or just plain selfish. He probably knew something of her sexual history from Nadine. On which I have no intention of expanding, thought Stella. Nothing to do with him, really, any of this. But he's a decent enough chap and one confidence deserves another, I suppose. If confidence is the right word.

'Nadine envied you,' said Richard abruptly.

Stella was almost shocked. She stared at him, momentarily thrown.

He qualified. 'Not in the absolute sense. And not that she was in any way dissatisfied with her own lot. She just saw you as having something she didn't – experience, opportunity . . .' He let the sentence trail away.

Yes, thought Stella. That fits. And somehow I never noticed at the time.

*

'There's a man,' says Nadine. This is not a question but a statement. She looks at Stella across a table in the cafeteria of the Royal Academy after the exhibition visit which has been the pretext for their meeting. They have not seen each other for over a year.

'Well . . . yes,' says Stella. She would rather not go into the matter, but sees that there is no escape.

Nadine contemplates her. 'I've known for the last hour. It's written all over you. You've got that sort of feverish look.' She sounds almost grumpy, and if Stella was not in this state of floating detachment, she would have detected then the whiff of envy. Nadine feels sidelined, high and dry on her island of marriage and maternity, while Stella is still out there in the world – free, in love. But Stella is for once blinkered, she is barely seeing or hearing Nadine. She is indeed in love. This means that she is self-absorbed, unobservant and not herself at all.

'Is he an anthropologist?'

'No . . . no, he's a journalist.'

Nadine is even more put out. An anthropologist would have staid, pedestrian connotations. To her ears journalist sounds racy, even glamorous. She is thinking that Stella always had more dashing men than she did. But Stella has not got the Georgian farmhouse in Sevenoaks and the two gorgeous children. And probably this man won't last.

'Where did you meet him?'

'Oh . . . in Malta. I did a field study there this summer.'

Malta. Sun, brown skin, hot nights. Beaches. Damn her, thinks Nadine, who is no longer enjoying her day out.

*

Feeling disagreeably bloated, Stella watched Richard attend to the bill, which was delivered discreetly disguised as a leather notepad.

'Thank you for a splendid meal,' she said. 'A treat.'

'It's for me to thank you. You did us proud.'

I do not know how this has come about, thought Stella. How can it be that by some diabolical trick I am sixty-five and sitting in a sugar pink restaurant with the husband of my old friend Nadine, who is not anywhere at all. How has it come to this?

'You will be the talk of the local history group for months. Our meetings are seldom so colourful.'

And how did I come to be trying to explain the seminal matter of cultural difference to fifteen oddly assorted people in something called a village hall?

'A pleasure,' she said. 'Rather cursory treatment of a hefty subject, I'm afraid. I did try to beef up the travel aspect, as you suggested.'

They rose from the table. A waiter eased Stella into her coat as though he were robing a bishop. Outside the restaurant, she turned to Richard.

'I don't think Nadine envied me, exactly. We shot off in different directions. Having shared a starting-line, as it were. The thought could be unsettling.'

He shrugged, smiled. 'Maybe. Whatever . . . she came to see you as a symbol of lost promise, I think. Her lost promise.'

'She would have hated to live as I have. What she had was what she always wanted.'

'Oh, undoubtedly,' said Richard. 'But that doesn't necessarily induce absolute satisfaction, does it?'

Stella drove home through a black velvet night, under a sky

crackling with stars. The night sky was clear in these parts, quite unlike the orange pall that hangs over cities. The weather was more vivid, you were more acutely aware of sun and rain, of the theatrical range of cloud effects, from incandescent back-lit masses to the delicate Wedgwood veil of summer cirrus. The car's headlights made a golden tunnel of the lanes down which she drove; when she came out into the open the hills were a long flank against the sparkling sky. Darkness everywhere, except for the flare of some vehicle on a road. An uninhabited landscape, you would think, if you did not know of its intricate, intimate layers of community.

And invisible populace. She thought of the force-lines out there – of tacit understanding, of mutual incomprehension, of tolerance, of hostility. Those who operated in shiftless isolation, those locked into networks of mutual aid and dependence. An untidy place, she thought. An African village is a miracle of cohesion, by comparison.

North Somerset Herald

Tarantulas on Show

The South West Tarantula Society's summer show at Tropical World near Taunton on Sunday attracted around 100 entries in seven categories.

Hoccombe Market

17 July's Hoccombe Market saw 391 fat lambs meet an easier trade to average 109.4 pence, selling to a top price of 48.50, 123.00 pence a kilo. 59 killing ewes sold to a steadier trade, half-meat ewes to 34.00, plain to 25.50, killing rams to 45.00.

Puppy Show, Clapperton

The Clapperton Foxhounds Puppy Show was held on 10 July at the Kennels, West Oxton, by invitation of the Joint Master. Five couples of doghounds and two couples of bitches were then judged. After the Puppy Show everyone adjourned to enjoy a splendid tea, most kindly provided by the Masters, who then presented prizes to the puppy walkers.

Minehead Rubbish-Bin Fire

Firefighters were called out to a blaze in a rubbish-bin on the esplanade. The fire had spread to a neighbouring seat and lamp-post, which were badly damaged.

Local History Group Meeting a Success

The West Somerset local history group was entertained by slides and a talk given by Miss Stella Brentwood, who recalled her days as an anthropologist. A lively discussion followed. The group's next meeting will be on 9 September.

Chapter Eight

Stella had named the dog. A dog must be summoned, therefore it needs a name. She found the choice exasperatingly difficult, seeking to avoid both the arch and the mundane. Persistent guilt about the creature's desperate devotion made her feel that she owed him at the least a carefully considered handle. Eventually she called him Bracken, remembering that her parents had a dog of that name, long ago in her adolescence. That animal was now reduced to a vaguely distasteful memory of something square and brown perpetually slumped on the hearthrug, but never mind. To bestow upon this new dog a name with ancestral overtones was a compliment and confirmation of status. She felt a mite less guilty.

Within a week she discovered that she had committed a minor solecism.

'What's that you've called that dog of yours?' enquired the postman, as she tried to keep the dog from assaulting him in frenzied propitiation.

'Bracken.'

The postman laughed. 'Hound name, that is. In these parts. You only get hounds called that. Better take care you keep him inside when the hunt's exercising.'

Stella had grown up in Enfield, where fox-hunting is not rife. She decided that it was hardly worth mentioning this in mitigation. The postman was an invaluable source of information; the occasional firm correction was a fair price. And so far as the name went, it was too late now. The dog already recognized his label. I'm sorry, Stella told him. Put it down to my suburban upbringing. We'll just have to keep this as a matter between ourselves.

And what about the postman himself, with his name from the Welsh valleys? Stella had presumed once to ask him if his forebears had come over the water to the mines up on the hill. He had shrugged. Didn't know. Didn't much care. That was then, this is now. Suffice it that he was of this place, and knew what was what. Unlike some.

Names, names . . . she thought. The ultimate signifier for those of us who like to ferret away at such things. Inside the cottage were card indexes and notebooks in which she had diligently recorded hundreds upon hundreds of names. These harvests could then be assembled into patterns – clusters of similar sounds which made kinship groupings and lineage structures. We all of us bear witness to our genes and are labelled accordingly. As a child she had been fascinated by the litany of the Old Testament – and Jared lived an hundred and sixty two years, and he begat Enoch . . . and Enoch lived sixty and five years, and begat Methuselah . . . She had savoured the outlandish names, chanting them aloud, noting the piling up of generation upon generation. Perhaps this early addiction counted for much.

But she had savoured also the names on the map of Greater London, noting how they appreciated in flavour from the muted streets and avenues and terraces of her own suburb to the metropolitan splendours of Trafalgar, Piccadilly, Victoria and Waterloo. She had compared her own homely no-frills

English family stock – Brentwoods on her father's side, Nordens on her mother's – with the more suggestive surnames of certain schoolmates. Elizabeth Cremona, whose father was Italian. The McTaggart sisters. May Chang. Fernanda Rodriguez. She approved such a freight of reference. What did Brentwood tell you, for heaven's sake?

She had learned about this landscape from its names. Topographical history left her somewhat cold, but she had borrowed the Somerset volume of *The Place-Names of England* from the library and become interested in the betraying dissection of the names of farms and villages. Here was the relentless Anglo-Saxon plod, there was a faint Celtic whisper. Here a hint of Roman, there a Norman reference. Nothing was arbitrary, each name a coded signal.

Similarly the more intimate surroundings, for each and every one of us. 'Don't need to be much of a detective to know you've spent time out of this country,' the removal foreman had said, perched on a pile of cases with a mug of tea in his hand, watching one of his henchmen carry in the big khelim rug, the Turkish brass tray. 'And all these books. Dead give-away.' He sat upon three book boxes, his feet upon another. He did not specify what it was that was given away, but the thought hung in the air. One kind of person as opposed to another.

The books were now unpacked, and continued to bear witness, as did the contents of Stella's desk, of the drawers of her bedroom chest. Possession of this, absence of these and those. We are defined by what we own, by what we are called.

'Come along then, you,' she said to the dog. 'Time for a walk.'

The favoured direction was always up the old mineral line.

94

The dog, too, now automatically headed that way. Once off the track over the field, you were on to the sheltered sunken lane which had once been the route of the railway incline and you could go as high and as far as you wished – on several occasions Stella had been right up to the ridge of the Brendons. Once in a while she would meet another walker, or someone on a horse, but for the most part the route was deserted. Knowing its original function, she found it impossible not to imagine the industrial bustle of that other time – the waggons grinding up and down the line, the gangs of miners at the winding-houses. But if you knew nothing of this, the place was just an agreeable and apparently fortuitous path for a country walk.

Stella thought of the miners today, as she walked between hedgebanks that rippled with birdsong. She saw them in the mind's eye in monochrome, an effect prompted presumably by old sepia photographs – short dark men done up in that complicated garb of the Victorian working man which is a parody of respectable dress: the battered jacket, the waistcoat, the scarf at the neck, the cap. Talking Welsh, presumably. Conspicuous and alien. Immigrants. Nothing left of them today but this track, a scattering of Baptist chapels and the postman, who was not interested in his ancestry. Fair enough. It is perhaps only the nicely adjusted who can afford to dismiss their antecedents. Those passionately interested in their roots are usually either the historically oppressed or the oppressors, both needing to prove a point.

Today she went only as far as the waterfall, where the track briefly ran parallel with a stream just as it tumbled down over rocks set in woodland. Bracken had a drink. Stella rested on a fallen tree and then headed back.

Coming out on to the lane she saw the Hiscox boys with their bikes propped up against the hedgebank. They squatted alongside, examining a wheel. Hearing her step, they turned and abruptly stood up. Bracken, running ahead, approached and sniffed tentatively at one of the pairs of grubby jeans, his ears laid back ingratiatingly. At once the boy shoved at him with his foot – something nearer a kick than a push: 'Fuck off!'

Stella was jolted. The harsh adolescent voice hung in the bright morning. The dog had retreated to her side and she slipped on his lead. 'He wasn't going to hurt you. He's just curious.'

'I don't like dogs.'

'Really?' said Stella. 'Well, some don't, I suppose. He's the first I've had, as it happens.'

The boys stared at her. They were almost identical. Sun-burned sullen faces under mops of dark hair. Twins, you would have thought, except that one was slightly taller. With one accord they turned their backs on her and squatted down to the bikes again.

'Puncture?' said Stella determinedly. 'In my day it was that palaver with a bucket of water, looking for the bubbles. No doubt the technology has improved.'

Silence. Then the bigger boy swung his head fractionally in her direction and mumbled something.

'Sorry?'

'Piss off, will you? We're busy.'

The following things are in the drawers of Stella's desk. It is a pine knee-hole desk of no particular distinction, topped with a rectangle of imitation leather embossed in gilt.

Brown envelopes labelled Orkney, Malta, Nile Delta, Miscellaneous. These envelopes contain photographs. Some of the photographs are scenic, others show groups of people. Occasionally these groups include Stella. Other incarnations of Stella. She stands under a palm tree, flanked by beaming men in galabiehs. A tanned Stella wearing a large straw hat poses with a black-clad priest in front of a baroque church. She perches, laughing, on the seat of a tractor; a big man with a mane of ginger hair leans with his hand on the steering wheel, like a groom curbing a stationary horse.

An assortment of card-index boxes in varying degrees of decay. These are the boxes which are filled with names. Packed, stuffed, crammed with names. They are a distillation of humanity, these boxes, a reduction of flesh and blood and bone into a compact mass of cards, $5'' \times 8''$. There are hundreds upon hundreds of people in here. Pietru and Victor and Pawlu and Maddalena and Tereza. Ahmed and Saleh and Fawzia and Fatima. Neil and Isobel and Mary and Fergus. They are bleached, shrunk, stripped of life and stashed away here as silent witness to patterns of human behaviour.

A string of blue beads.

A bundle of letters, tied with string. The letters are all addressed to Stella in the same hand but the provenance is global. Smudgy illegible postmarks from goodness knows where, clumps of gaudy stamps.

A stack of notebooks, also labelled: Orkney, Nile Delta, Malta. And Birmingham, Sheffield, Milton Keynes.

Several passports in Stella's name. The corners are cut off to indicate that they are out of date, the pages are liberally spattered with immigration stamps.

*

These things are on, in or around a large deal table with a single long drawer in a small room adjoining the sitting-room in the Hiscox bungalow. Karen Hiscox refers to this room as her office.

A metal spike on which is impaled a column of bills, many inches high. Electricity and telephone bills are almost invariably in red: second demands.

A packet of rat poison.

A stack of back issues of the *North Somerset Herald*.

A tin of flea powder.

A calendar for 1989, turned to the May page, showing a woodland vista, with bluebells. This item hanging from a hook on the wall.

A shotgun. Also hanging from a hook.

A battered wooden box with hinged lid, which looks as though it may once have housed a croquet set. Inside the box are a dog collar and lead, a Johnny Walker whisky bottle (empty), several cartridge cases (full), a large torch with no glass or bulb, a bundle of bank statements, a lipstick, packets of Disprin and Elastoplast, a bulldog clip holding three documents, one recording the birth of Michael John Picton, another that of Peter Keith Picton, and the last notifying Edward James Picton that he has been declared bankrupt. There are also Twix and Mars Bar wrappers, loose change, pieces of string, torn stamps and assorted further detritus.

In the Hiscox bungalow, in the bottom drawer of the chest in Gran's room, there is a knitting bag. Inside the bag are knitting needles and the half-finished sleeve of some blue garment, grimy with age, still on the needles, along with various hanks and balls of wool, these, too, old and grubby. There are also some knitting patterns, rolled up together and held by an elastic band.

Within the core of this knitting pattern tube are other items. The estate agent's particulars for a house in Kingston-upon-Thames, called the Larches, with four bedrooms, sitting-room opening on to a conservatory and a half acre of landscaped gardens.

A letter. The letter is on thin lined notepaper and is dated 11 February 1986. It is apparently minus the last page.

Dear Milly: It's not my business, I dare say, but I feel I've got to speak out. I tried to ring you the other day and got Karen. Told me you were out. At half past nine in the evening? I said, Milly never goes out after dark. Then she became offensive and I put the phone down. Milly, Karen has been trouble from the word go, frankly, and if she were my daughter, I'd make it plain enough's enough. You and Arthur did everything for her any child could ask and a fat lot of gratitude you've had. If she and Ted have bitten off more than they can chew with this garage business and come a cropper, then it's up to them to pick themselves up as best they can. They've no right calling on you to bale them out. Your home's your own, Milly. Arthur would have been horrified. He died easy, knowing you were comfortably set up. Well, not easy, given he was only fifty-six, but easier, put it that way. As for Karen saying you'll be better off with them in any case, let me just point out that Karen's not the easiest person in the world to get along with and you should know that better than anyone. Look after you, she says, does she? That'll be the first time I've ever heard of that young woman looking after anybody except number one. I don't like the sound of this, Milly, and since I doubt if anyone else is going to say so loud and clear, I'm doing just that. It's my duty as your sister, that's how I see it, though I dare say you won't thank me. And if Karen and that Ted . . .

That woman had come out of the field when they were trying to fix Peter's broken spoke. She'd come up suddenly so it took them by surprise, and then the bloody dog started sniffing around. So Peter kicked it. Afterwards they both wished he'd kicked it harder, but it felt good at the time as it was. And Michael told her to piss off and that was good too.

Stupid cow. What business was it of hers? Asking a stupid question like that.

If we had proper bikes, they told each other. Decent bikes like other people got.

They sat in their place behind the sheds and worked themselves up about the bikes. If we say to her we'll do without our birthdays and Christmas. We'll muck out the pens every day, after school. Half an hour or so of this and they'd got up enough head of steam to ask. She'd been in quite a good mood the last few days anyway.

She was in the room she called her office. Where the gun was. She was sitting at the table where she put bills and stuff, sorting through a pile of papers.

They stood at the door. Even just looking at her they knew it wouldn't be any good. The way her mouth was screwed up into a hard knot. The good mood was over, for some reason.

'Clear off, I haven't got time for you.'

Peter said, 'Mum . . .'

She slammed the papers down on the table. 'Didn't you hear what I said? D'you want me to say it again? Louder? Longer?'

They went.

She'd be doing the accounts. That stuff with piles of figures and bits of paper. Their father wasn't any good at that and she was. She'd been to business school, way back, she said. And before they were born their parents had the garage, they'd had people working under them, there'd been a turnover of thousands. She had plenty of business experience, more than any of these people around here. Her in the village shop. The farm people they dealt with. They're rubbish, she said. Just you remember that, if anyone tries to come it with you. Remember we've been in business in a bigger way than they've ever dreamed of.

There was nothing, absolutely nothing, got her rag more than people not reckoning with who she was. Like the man from the farm shop, that time.

The farm shop was nothing to do with any farm, really. It was just a shop. On the main road, where cars could pull in, selling fruit and veg and a lot of other things. The man had come to see if their mother would like to be one of his egg suppliers. Eggs and maybe frozen rabbit pieces. He'd said a price and apparently that had been OK, because she had him in and they'd sat talking half an hour or more and you'd have thought they were getting on like a house on fire. Presumably the man thought that. And then, right at the end when he was going, he made a mistake. He said, 'By the way, I've got a vacancy for a part-time salesperson if you'd be interested. One of the girls left to have a baby. Be nice to have you in the shop.'

That did it. She went all stiff but he didn't notice. Got into his car and went.

And then she blew up. 'Just who does he bloody well think he is? Who does he bloody well think *I* am? Part-time bloody salesperson! I've *owned* a shop bigger than he's got.'

They backed her up. Michael said, 'Stupid git. He'd got no business, talking like that. Silly bugger.'

Later, Peter said, 'Was it a farm shop, Mum?'

'Was what?'

'The shop you had, that was bigger than that man's?'

'I don't know what you're talking about.'

So they shut up about that. Maybe she'd meant that garage. Where they had half a dozen people working for them and a turnover of thousands.

When the man came back later in the week, thinking to pick up the eggs and the rabbit pieces, she let him have it. She stood with her hands on her hips as he got out of the car, saying nothing. She let him start talking, start saying things about the eggs.

She said, 'What eggs?'

He'd stopped being all cheery by now. The smile wiped off his face all right. He went on again about the eggs. And the frozen rabbit pieces.

She let fly at him. She bawled at him that if he thought he could pull a fast one on her he had another think coming and she traded where she chose thank you very much and he needn't think he could come down here acting like Lord Muck just because he'd got a tacky little business flogging a few rotten cabbages.

She kept it up the way she could, on and on, and the man stood there gobsmacked and beginning to get angry himself, you could see. When she stopped for a moment he began: 'Now, look here, Mrs Hiscox . . .'

The boys had come up to stand just behind their mother. Michael said, 'Don't you talk to my mother like that, you stupid git.'

The man turned round and walked to his car. He got in and slammed the door. He didn't hear her shouting at him to get away from her and not come back because he was revving the engine and crashing the gears as he backed out on to the track.

A week or so later they had seen the man from the farm shop in Minehead, when they were taking Gran to the bank. Their mother was in the supermarket. The man saw them, too. He stopped and stared. Then he said, 'I know you, don't I?'

They started to move away.

'You're Mrs Hiscox's boys.'

'Mind your own business,' said Michael. The man was standing in front of him, blocking his way.

'As disagreeable a woman as I've come across. And you could do with a lesson in manners yourself.'

'Piss off.'

'The same to you, young man. But first of all you can give a message to your mother. You can tell her . . .'

They elbowed past the man and took off round the corner. In the car they told her about what had happened.

'So I said to him, piss off.'

'That's right. Show him he can't mess with us. He wants taking down a peg or two, that man.'

Peter said, 'We told him any time he comes near our place again he'll get a punch on the nose.'

She laughed.

'So he backs off. We're stood there and he scarpers. Suppose he thought we were going to give it to him right then.'

She laughed again. 'You want bangers and mash for your tea?'

All that was months ago. They hadn't seen the man again

but every time their mother drove past the farm shop she accelerated and you could tell she was all charged up. She'd take it out on whatever got in her way next – another car, or the girl at the check-out in the supermarket. Or them, if they weren't careful.

Chapter Nine

One day Stella identified a social anthropologist's paradise. Unfortunately, this scientific treasure was unreachable, sealed away in the nineteenth century. The place that descended from it was still very much there – Watchet, a small port on the north coast of Somerset, with attractive harbour, esplanade and facilities for visitors by way of pubs, cafés and a car-park. But the alluring social structure that had brought a professional gleam to her eye was lost, gone, extinguished – reduced to a handful of names and some faded photographs in the water-front museum.

Time was, this place had hatched a highly specialized occupation. The earning of hobble by hobblers. Hobbling, this trade must presumably be called. Back then, the several kinds of vessel plying the Bristol Channel – the ketches and smacks and sloops – could be worked by a crew of only two or three, but when it came to navigating the awkward entrance to Watchet harbour for loading and unloading, more hands were needed. Accordingly, over generations, Watchet had supplied the need. Hobble boats, crewed by Watchet families, sailed out from the harbour to meet incoming vessels, negotiate a price and then bring the vessel in.

A sensible, pragmatic arrangement, convenient to all. Watchet earned a living; small craft were not obliged to carry a surplus crew. But by the mid-century the system had gone awry. It had run amok, betrayed by its own fatal internal flaw. The hobblers had succumbed to internecine warfare. The trade was now in the hands of just three families; the three rival boats were locked into self-destructive competition. In their efforts to be ahead of the game in learning when a vessel was approaching Watchet, members of the warring families roamed the cliffs, peering out to sea; they crept around the town at night to interrogate fishermen. They put to sea and skulked along the coast at Minehead or Porlock, hoping to intercept incoming craft – a precarious move which risked missing the quarry and returning to base to find her in the hands of the jubilant enemy. Things got physical. There was fighting in the narrow streets of Watchet.

What happened next is remarkable. The landlord of the town's principal inn, himself a master mariner, saw that not only was the situation ridiculous, but it lent itself to a fine and progressive solution. He summoned representatives of the three families and proposed the amalgamation of the three boats into a union of mutual benefit, to be known as the United Sailors' Society. Rules, regulations, monthly meetings, the keeping of accounts. Equal distribution of funds to all members. Provision for sickness and pension payments, for widows' benefits. Not to mention the interesting possibilities of co-operation in the fixing of a hobble fee unimpeded by the rate-cutting of rival service providers. The masters of the vessels working that coast must have shuddered when news of this *entente cordiale* reached their ears.

At this point the story of the Watchet hobblers becomes a matter for labour and trade union historians and Stella lost interest. What I want is a word with these families, she thought.

Some good in-depth interviews. Not to mention a careful examination of lineage structures. I want to know exactly what Wedlakes, Allens and Pittaways thought of one another, and what happened if a young Wedlake lad fancied an Allen girl, and how the women coped with a situation of prohibited relationships. I want to know how the hobble war affected the extended community. I want to get dug into Watchet of the 1840s, with a notebook and a card index, and act as a pair of eyes and ears. First time I've ever thought there might be something to be said for time travel. What a scoop I'd have! The television people would be all over me. Prime-time documentary on BBC 2: 'This remarkable account of drama and tension in an isolated and forgotten society by one of today's most innovative anthropologists . . .'

She came out of the museum and sat looking at the little harbour. Not a very serious harbour, these days. A few fishing boats. Otherwise just some distinctly unbusinesslike dinghies and motorboats and the promise of day trips to Lundy or Ilfracombe.

Stella knew this place already. Not the museum, which seemed to be a relatively recent installation. But she had sat precisely here, looking at this view of boats beached in low-tide mud with the grey-brown sea beyond and the grey-blue sky above that. She had eaten fish and chips at the café on the esplanade. She had walked on the cliffs beyond the town.

They had. The two of them. It was possible, all things considered, that she had been happier in this place than ever before or since. Here, she had cruised briefly in that stratosphere which is beyond normal emotion, beyond contentment or exhilaration, that condition which drenches all perception at the time but is only recognizable in retrospect.

Happiness being notoriously irretrievable, she could do no more today than pay respectful tribute to that *alter ego*. She had wondered if it would be a treacherous experience, to revisit this place, but in the event the treachery seemed in a curious way to be her own response. She had been almost at once distracted by wandering into the museum and falling upon the provocative story of the hobblers. And now, watching bickering gulls and a dog rooting in a dustbin and a boy fishing from the pier – just as the two of them probably had done back then – there was no anguish, just a contemplation: vivid, enduring.

'Anywhere so long as it's rural and blindingly English,' he had said, on a phone that crackled and whistled in a way that international calls no longer do. So she had booked in at a pub that did bed and breakfast in a village that was unfamiliar but which should do nicely, according to the road atlas. She had met him at Heathrow and they had driven straight there, to the double bed in a room looking out on to a steeply tipping hillside, where sheep grazed on ledges and stared in at them.

The next day they visited Watchet. It was a cool grey autumn day; they both wore sweaters and jackets. In the weeks since she last saw him she had thought of him always in hot weather clothes, bare-armed, tanned. To see him otherwise both startled and stimulated her. It was as though he suddenly displayed some new facet of his personality. I don't really know him at all, she thought. I am in love with him, but that is quite another matter.

He was a foreign correspondent for one of the broadsheet newspapers. She had met him on a rock off the coast of Malta.

A rock to which you swam from a cove known, on the whole, only to connoisseurs. She had been sitting on this rock and a man had pulled himself out of the water and come to sit beside her. He had said his name was Dan Mitchell. He talked. And she had stopped being irritated at his invasion of her rock because his talk was intriguing. It was not the expatriate conversation to which she had become accustomed. He was not interested in decent restaurants or sailing excursions. He talked about the place and its people. When, later, she played back what had been said between them, she saw that it had been a subtle process of negotiation which she had not recognized at the time. He had probed her for responses and picked up direction and inclination from what she had said. He had talked about the Maltese language, she had pointed out that the origin is Arabic and had given some instances. He moved on to village names and topography and thus, after half an hour, sitting there between the sea and the sun, he had nailed her for who she was and what she did, while she knew that he was based in Italy and was here to cover an international summit conference about to take place on the island. It was the sixties, when summit conferences were all the rage. She had ceased to wonder how he was aware of this bathing cove known only to connoisseurs, because she realized that he was the sort of person who at once, by some osmotic process, knows what ought to be known about an unfamiliar place. They had swum back together to the cove and as they got into their cars he asked her where she was living. She told him. The next day he turned up in the village.

The summit conference ended and he left the island. Ten days later he was back. Italy is no great distance from Malta; if a busy journalist decides to take a break, he may as well take it there as anywhere. And so it went, for the rest of that summer. She lived on two different planes: work in the village, and the times when he was there.

In Watchet he said, 'This place could rate as the opposite of Malta. Like the reverse of a coin. How about us? Are we the same?'

She was fresh from the night before. That double bed. Him. The impassive sheep.

'So it would seem.' And she laughed – a jubilant, carefree laugh that took in the night and the past months and this moment and whatever there might be to come.

'I am not a good proposition,' he had told her. 'You do realize that? It will always be like this.'

Oh, yes, she knew he was not a good bet. He lived with his bags packed, at the beck and call of events. It would always be like this and she had no option but to go along with it, because we do not choose with whom we fall in love. I am sentenced to this, she thought. Not that I would wish it otherwise. He will vanish, and reappear. Or not, as the case may be. Arrangements will be made and then broken. I shall wonder, as I wonder now, if possibly he has another woman somewhere else.

'But then you're not exactly rooted yourself, are you? What's the longest you've ever lived under one roof?'

Stella pondered. A year, she decided. Definitely she had chalked up a year.

'There you are, then.'

She did not know what he meant by this. We are not suited? We are kindred spirits? They had been blown together, on a rock. In the societies she studied, sexual liaisons sprang from associations that were generations deep. She and Dan Mitchell had barely a common acquaintance. They shared nothing except the past months.

He was a man charged with energy – restless, inquisitive. The energy seemed to focus in his eyes – brilliant, interrogative eyes that fixed on you as though you were the only person of any interest to him. Brown eyes in a sharp-featured face on which a smile seemed only just held back. A smile of wry amusement, of disbelief. A charismatic personality, she realized, having seen many such in many societies. And he came and went with the immediacy of an apparition. He was nowhere in sight, and then suddenly he was beside you. He was in the room, and then all at once he was not. Just as he had slid up from the sea on to that rock – sleek and smiling and unheralded by so much as a splash.

He never accounted for himself. He never said where he had been or where he was going. Simply, he came and went.

He did not talk about his past. From time to time something emerged – incidentally, it seemed, woven by accident into whatever he had been saying, so that only afterwards would Stella realize that she had learned something about him: he had been at a major public school which he held in contempt; he spoke Russian as well as French, German and Italian; he had a child, a boy of ten.

Hardly a matter for wonder, she told herself. The man is forty. Naturally, he has been around. As have I. All the same, she found herself wondering. Not about the boy, but about the mother.

Walking on the cliffs beyond Watchet, she asked him. Idly, as though it were neither here nor there.

She was German, it seemed. Inge. She lived in Cologne,

with Konrad, the boy. Dan visited. Sometimes he took Konrad on trips.

'We've never been married,' he said. He knew her thoughts, Stella saw, and felt exposed. He smiled. 'Water under the bridge, except for Konrad.'

They had eaten fish and chips in the café on the esplanade and then walked on the cliffs. They scrambled down the cliff path on to a beach and saw that the cliffs were seamed with pink alabaster. They held hands. They stood in the wind and kissed. Others steered clear of them. We look like what we are, Stella thought. Lovers. People are wary of lovers, for good reason. They recognize an abnormal state of mind, and stay away. They see a temporary madness. They see those who care for nothing but themselves, who are immune to the rest of the world.

This will never do, she thought. That is what I know, even in the midst of it. And I don't care. I know that it will all end in tears, more likely than not, and still I cannot care. It is enough to be here, now. To have had these weeks and months. To feel thus.

The first time he came to the Maltese village she had had to ask him never to come there again. He parked his hired car in the square and made enquiries. By the time he reached the house where she lived and worked, he had a Pied Piper following of children and there were watching eyes on every doorstep and at every window.

He was contrite. 'I'm sorry. Can't you put it about that I'm a colleague? Come to give a helping hand with . . .' he cast an eye over her table . . . 'lists.' He picked up a sheet of paper and stared. 'Lists of what?'

'Makes of firework,' said Stella.

He sat down, uninvited. 'Tell me.'

So she told him. About the firework *festas* which dominate the lives of Maltese villages, about the warring band clubs and the allegiances to rival saints. Outside, the narrow street became unaccountably busy. Various neighbours dropped by to see if by any chance Stella needed eggs, sugar, a loaf of bread. Eventually she said, 'I'm sorry, but really I'm afraid you'll have to go. I'll never live this down.'

He was further contrite. 'I do so much barging in the course of business, I forget to be sensitive.' He rose and stood looking at her. 'So what do I do to reach you? I can see there's no phone here.'

She knew then how it was going to be. When he had gone she could still feel his look upon her, like the touch of a hand on the skin. She was exhilarated. She was horrified. A field trip was sacred territory. She did not see how she could work and have a love affair at the same time. Thus it was that she came to live two lives, over that summer: the village life and that other life.

In the village she became an expert on makes of firework. This was necessary in order to note the preparations for and rate of expenditure on the *festas* in honour of saints' days around which the village year revolved. Several times a year the village exploded. It erupted in a shower of flares and sparks, clouds of acrid smoke and a few hours of deafening bangs. Thus did the rival band clubs honour their chosen saint and assert superiority not only over opposing saints but also over neighbouring villages, who might have cut corners on expense and thus banged to less effect. Within the village, allegiance to the two or three different band clubs split the place several ways. Male members of families decided on their allegiance in adolescence, and henceforth devoted themselves to their chosen patron. On their saint's *festa* day they strutted the streets in the band and later toured the island in buses and battered cars, letting off firecrackers and shouting the superiority of both saint and village. A system which channelled male aggression and *esprit de corps* in much the same way as loyalty to football teams does in other societies. And of course it suited the church nicely, focusing funds and attention on both the institution and its physical expression, the great baroque presence in the central square.

The village priest was Stella's confidant and informant. Once convinced of her scholarly status and that she was nothing to do with the government (anthropologists are suspected of being disguised spies of authority, the world over), he was prepared to brief and help her. He guided her through the complex network of familial relationships. He told her who worked where and who subscribed to which saint. Many of the cards in the index boxes in Stella's desk bore entries in his neat, seminarian hand. He acted as translator when necessary.

The Maltese village had eerie affinities with that Nile Delta village on which she had cut her professional teeth. Once again, she lived in close proximity to a family. The rooms she rented opened on to the interior courtyard in which they kept the rabbits and chickens which supplemented the father's earnings as a dockyard worker in Valletta. Once again, she was drawn into the life of the neighbourhood and had to struggle to retain her detachment. And, once again, she was a woman.

The priest could reconcile her role and her gender because she was not a Catholic and was thus outside his remit. She both did not count and had to be accounted for differently. A lifestyle that would not do at all for a local woman was acceptable because Stella became in his eyes a sort of honorary man, by virtue of her occupation. The village recognized her as a woman, with all that that implied. The wives, mothers, daughters and grandmothers found her accordingly more approachable, but were concerned about her lack of husband or children. The men were wary, both fearing to be compromised if they associated too closely with her and feeling that she couldn't possibly appreciate male concerns in any case. The priest became an essential mediator.

The incursion of Dan Mitchell threatened her precarious neutrality. If she was observed to be courted by a man, the village would be enthralled, but her status would be radically changed. The priest would take her less seriously. Everyone else would see her as all too interestingly flesh and blood in a way that would impede her working relationships.

Dan perfectly understood. He was amused, conspiratorial. He enjoyed the furtive quality of their meetings, as though the village were some heavy Victorian father from whom she slipped away. They met in Valletta bars, in the restaurant in Mdina, at favourite assignation points on cliffs and by coves and beaches reached only along rough tracks. Sometimes she came to the hotel in which he stayed, and then drove back late in the hot starry night, creeping guiltily into the village, fearing that her comings and goings must be noted. She invented friends and outside commitments, avoiding the eye of the priest and the family with whom she lodged. My old school friend who is staying in Mdina. The tennis club.

The island became a place of wonder. Previously, she had seen it as an overcrowded landscape of cluttered villages set amid scrubby fields. Prickly pears seemed the predominant vegetation, the architecture echoed blockhouses. Tourists and British expatriates whooped it up on the beaches and in the Valletta bars. Now, it became suffused with private perceptions, their shared discoveries. The cliffs from which you looked down on to a quilted sea. The narrow ancient streets of Mdina, with glimpses into private courtyard gardens. Dolphin door knockers. The harbour-front bar where you could eat grilled swordfish. The island's deep extended past: the mad tenacity of the crusader knights, the dark impenetrable hints of prehistory. Stella saw the familiar faces of her village in a new light, recognizing their tenuous descent from these things.

She worked all the better for this heightened state of mind. She was around the village each morning at five or six, when the women went out on the first of their many daily shopping excursions. She sat up late each night over her cards and notebooks. She was filled with purpose and well-being. I should have done this before, she thought. Lined up a love affair for each field trip.

She never knew when he would come, or if he was already there. The proprietor of the village bar, who took telephone messages and served as substitute for a public phone, would send his son to her. For ever after, the sight of that child's small brown face peering round her door would come to mind as the signal of delight. He would hand her a screw of paper, beaming, knowing that whatever it was he brought was something rich and precious. His father's careful, laboured hand: 'Miss Stella to telephone please Xara Palace Hotel.' There was never any name. She knew who it was she had to telephone. She rewarded the small boy with sweeties or a bottle of Tizer and they glowed at one another.

The island burned under the summer sky. Stella measured time not in days or weeks but in terms of his arrivals and departures. It was June when first they met. One day she saw on the calendar in the village bar that it was now August and was startled – that so little time should have passed, and so much. His visits melded into one continuous experience, yet each was distinguished by something they did, something seen, something said. The time when they swam in the darkness off a deserted beach, with the car headlights making long funnels of light across the sand and into the water. The time she sat waiting for him in a café, savouring the pleasure of expectation, watching, intent on picking him out in the crowded street – and then turned to find him sitting alongside her, silent and smiling, himself the watcher.

The time they quarrelled about human nature. Facing each other over a red checked tablecloth and the remains of a meal. Exterior, night. Insects battering the light-bulbs slung from a vine above their heads.

'So what have you learned from your village?' says Dan. His inquisitorial style. This could grate, occasionally.

'A great deal about firework manufacture and the range of Catholic saints,' Stella reflects. 'And that people – these people at any rate – can live in remarkable harmony.'

'You surprise me.'

'They set great store by getting on with each other. They don't like to fall out with neighbours.'

'What about these feuding band clubs?'

'Just a way of channelling off aggressive inclinations. It seems to work. Homicide is virtually unknown in Malta.'

Dan raises an eyebrow. 'And all this inter-village sparring you describe?'

'A further means of cementing loyalties within particular villages – a harmless form of us against them that firms up neighbourly feeling.'

'Some might say it's blood lust held in check by the forces of the law.'

'I don't think so,' says Stella, who is now becoming riled. She recognizes that she is identifying with the village, which is a touch unprofessional, and so she is annoyed also with herself.

'I can't share your benign view of human nature,' says Dan. 'I've just come from Sicily – sussing out the Mafia. Now there's a subject for you: "Kinship and Obligation in *Cosa Nostra*".'

'I don't think I'll take it on, thank you.'

'Too right, you wouldn't last a week.'

Stella lets this pass. 'My view isn't entirely benign. But there's plenty of evidence that, given the opportunity, people prefer to be accommodating. It's expedient, apart from anything else. Be nice to others and they're more likely to be nice to you.'

'Tell that to the thugs in Palermo.'

'Groups like that are an aberration,' says Stella crossly.

'Well, if they are, then they're a very effective one,' he retorts. 'And a global phenomenon, what's more.'

'Anthropologically speaking, they fly in the face of the general tendency,' says Stella. Possibly she sounds a touch didactic. Possibly he thinks so.

'Well,' says Dan, 'I'm just a hack observer of how people carry on, and I say there's a ripe capacity out there for depraved treatment of others.'

And so on – over the wine, under the stars. Until they declared truce and went back to Dan's hotel to settle their differences in bed.

This exchange lurks in Stella's mind as she walks again on the beach of alabaster, alone. What is in her head is a rich mix of precision and effect. Words and phrases and exact recoveries are superimposed upon a hazy background of sights and scenes and voices. The great cacophony of what has happened, with its mysterious, abiding, insistent notes. But what seemed most significant of all, now, was the inexorable way in which that time was wound into this. She owed her presence here, today, to that summer. Out of it sprang the time in Somerset with Dan Mitchell. Because of that she was here again now, contemplating the shade of her former self, but less concerned with that lurking presence than with the even more unreachable affairs of some nineteenth-century boatmen.

Chapter Ten

The procurement of food is an activity of social significance in all societies. From hunting and gathering to shopping. In the Maltese village, where few people had fridges and food perished fast, the women paid five or six visits a day to the various suppliers. On each occasion they exchanged news and views and checked up on what was going on. Similarly in the Nile Delta. Working in the inner cities of the eighties Stella had noted the blow struck by supermarkets to this crucial conduit of communication. The corner shop puts up a brave struggle, but it has lost its significant status.

In Somerset much the same applied, except that local establishments still had some clout as centres for the exchange of information and opinion. It was this that drew Stella frequently to the general grocery in the village nearest to the cottage, where prices were high and choice restricted. She had always seen shopping as an essential daily move for reasons over and beyond the need to get hold of some food.

The general store was called a Minimart and sold nothing whatsoever of local provenance. What was on sale could have been found in Salford, Brixton or Glasgow, and a good deal of it in Boston, Singapore or Adelaide. The proprietor, on the other hand, was a product of the place. Her family name reverberated across the pages of local newspapers and on the gravestones in the churchyard. A brisk forty-something, known to all as Molly, she presided from behind the till, darting out to find things for feckless customers or to replace goods dislodged by small children. It was neither possible nor expedient to complete any transaction without a conversation.

'So are you feeling properly dug in here now?'

'I am indeed,' says Stella. 'I've even lost track of how long it's been.'

'A couple of months, I'd say.' Molly pauses, considers one of Stella's purchases and rings it up on the till with deliberation. 'Lived in the country before, have you?'

'Well . . .' Stella thinks of the pulsating agricultural life of the Delta. She considers that Greek village, the stark sweep of the Orkney island. Country life? Of a sort, but not in the sense that Molly means. Molly's context is precise. Country life, to her, means a place like this — or rather, these specific westerly hills, these fields and villages. 'Not quite like round here.'

'Getting to know your neighbours?'

There is a hidden agenda here, Stella sees. She is supposed to say what she thinks of her neighbours. 'Everyone has been most welcoming,' she says, with stern neutrality.

'Of course you've got quite a mixed lot along the lane there now. John and Sue Morgan go way back, and Stan Watson. And the Laytons — not that I see much of them now, their daughter takes them into the Minehead supermarket once a week. Karen Hiscox comes in now and then, and those boys — not what you might call charmers those two, are they? Never a civil word. That Bristol family don't come in except for the Sunday papers. Had much to do with them?'

'Truth to tell,' says Stella, 'I haven't had a huge amount to do with anyone. I suppose I had imagined that rural life would be . . . more intimate.'

Molly rings up the last of Stella's purchases. 'Eight pounds forty.' Then she laughs. 'Intimate! Well, you could have said that once, I suppose. Where I grew up – and that's not a million miles from here – you knew everyone's business almost as well as they did themselves, if that's what you call intimate. And that was swings and roundabouts, know what I mean? Having the neighbours cheek by jowl isn't always an ideal situation, even if half of them are your second cousin once removed.' She laughs again. 'But you'll never have lived like that, I dare say, if it's towns you're used to.'

'People live like that in cities, too,' says Stella. 'At least some do.'

'Is that so?' Molly is clearly sceptical. And in any case another customer is looming. She sweeps Stella's purchases into a bag. 'There you go. Mind, we were all a bit more dependent on each other then, too. It's a bit different now.'

Stella thinks about this, driving home. True enough. A more detached attitude is a luxury of greater affluence and independence. If you are likely to need the help, guidance, support or co-operation of those around you, then you cannot afford such a cavalier approach. Neighbourliness thrives at subsistence level. The pioneer legacy is to be seen in the American tradition of hospitality and mutual obligation. You can afford to disregard the people next door only if certain that all your requirements will be supplied by neutral agencies. The doctor will come running if you are taken ill. The plumber and the electrician are at your beck and call. The garage mechanic will get your car to start. The money in your bank will cover all contingencies.

And only if your need for companionship and the occasional kind word are otherwise supplied, thought Stella. If you can pick up the phone to talk to a friend. If your personal community is far-flung, but easily accessible. As is mine. The self-contained capsule is a reasonable option, with the technology now available. Whether or not it is a desirable one is another matter.

It occurred to her that her first neighbour of all had been Nadine. The adjoining rooms on the top landing of that hefty red-brick Edwardian house on Banbury Road. The tap on the door while she was arranging her possessions – the Indian cotton bedspread draped over the bed, mugs and a biscuit tin on the shelf over the gas fire, her handful of books, her Picasso poster stuck to the wall. 'Hello – I'm Nadine from next door.'

So it all began, she thought. That moment, too, pointing directly to this, could one but have known it. Nadine led to Richard, who would one day send a Christmas card from west Somerset. And in between, of course, had been a lifetime of neighbour experience. Richer than most, probably, given Stella's peripatetic tendency. Many of her proximities had been grist to the professional mill. Those nearest to her in Orkney or the Delta or Birmingham had been neighbours and sometimes friends, but also indicators of behaviour and belief. She had been involved, but a part of her had also been neutral and detached, listening and observing.

She turned off the main road into the lane. The cottage was in view. Home? Did the heart lift at the sight of it? Did it soothe and reassure? Well, up to a point. There was a comfortable working relationship. And something more, perhaps – a stirring of proprietorial satisfaction. Mine. My property, my territory, the place where I am secure. There was a distant surge of feeling. Maybe this is it, she thought. Maybe I am growing roots for the first time ever, little white tendrilled fingers pushing down into the inviting red Somerset earth.

She'd been off somewhere – she didn't say where, she never said where she was going or how long she'd be – and when she got back she was in a rage. You could tell from the word go – the way she slammed the car door, banged into the house, didn't shout to say, 'You there? Michael? Peter?' She'd be spoiling for a fight, they knew that, so they stayed out of the way as long as they could.

Their father had been off on a job and came back later, so he didn't realize. At least not until it was too late. And he was in a bad mood himself. The sprayer had jammed with the job only half-done and he'd have to finish off tomorrow, when he'd fixed it.

It was different, when their father was in a mood. He didn't blow up like she did – go on for hours and then calm down all of a sudden and be like it hadn't happened. Their father would just go black silent and you'd better watch out, because he could stay like that for days on end, and when he was like that he'd do funny things. Sometimes you just heard him swearing and cursing by himself, out in the sheds. He might go to the pub and get pissed and end up having a set-to with someone. Anyone or anything that got in his way when he was in a mood, he'd go for. Back when they had that dog, the Staffordshire bull terrier bitch, when their mother thought she'd maybe do some dog breeding, back when that dog was around, their father'd take it out on her, beat the daylights out of her. The boys knew when to stay clear, but the stupid dog didn't, and she'd come smarming around and their father would get hold of her . . . It was dead funny, so long as you kept well away yourself.

So their father came in, grumbling about the sprayer. And then he went and asked when there'd be something to eat.

She hit the roof. Did he think she was some sort of skivvy? Did he think this was a McDonald's? She'd cook when she felt like it. Maybe soon, maybe not. Maybe not at all. If you want something to eat, you can bloody get it yourself. Did he think he was the only one round here who did a day's work? Did he think she had nothing to do but wait on him? I own this place, she said. I own this place more than you do. It's my money tied up in the business more than yours.

And so on. On and on. Not letting their father get a word in. Till the phone rang and she went to it and let whoever it was have an earful, and then their father had a chance when she banged the receiver down. He'd got his rag up now, too. The talk about her owning the place. He never liked that. Maybe it was true.

'I can't hear you,' she said. She clapped her hands over her ears and stood in front of him. 'Tra-la, tra-la, tra-la,' she said. 'I can't hear you. I'm not listening. I'm not interested. Got it? I'm not interested. Tra-la, tra-la, tra-la . . .'

And in the end their father slammed out of the house and off into the sheds. He'd be like thunder for days, probably. She might be as though nothing had happened, tomorrow, but not him.

You'd keep clear of him, if you knew what was good for you.

Stella had started to make a garden. She was clearing the overgrown and dishevelled rectangle around the cottage, having identified a lawn which had become a small hay field and old beds drowned in nettles and bindweed. She was surprised at herself. She knew nothing about gardening and did not consider herself particularly interested, but the physical activity was satisfying. Also, she supposed, she had succumbed to the proprietorial instinct. This was now hers, and could not be left in this disordered state. The previous owners of the cottage must have neglected the garden entirely. Its condition indicated an extended period of abandon. She knew nothing of them, except that they were a couple with a child who had owned the place for a year or two only and had moved out, leaving the cottage empty and in the hands of estate agents.

She recognized that her efforts were perfunctory and would be scorned by any serious gardener. She could not be bothered to consult books and the television programmes she occasionally noticed referred to situations of such abstract perfection as to be entirely incongruous. But there was a certain pleasure in reducing shrubs to a manageable size, clearing out nettles and cutting down the long grass. And each time she straightened up to take a breather there was that shapely landscape – the flowing lines of the hills with the sun highlighting an emerald field or a long, luminous streak of pink earth. Always the same but always different, like some theatre set endlessly transformed by ingenious effects of light to become drained and sombre, a palette of shadowy greens, or glowing with gold and rose and the running silver of wind on a field of corn.

It was the hills that did it, she thought, standing distracted with a pair of shears in her hand by the low hedge that shielded the front garden from the lane. The endlessly changing contours; the tipping fields and hedges that gave a sense of movement whichever way you looked. A trick of geology which infused the place with depth and distance, light and shadow. Aeons ago, the rocks heaved, and gave us this. And we are neither here nor there. Scratching briefly at the surface. Making fields. Digging ore. Trimming our natty little hedge. Beech, is this? Box? Privet? I should be better informed.

'*Gardening!*' said Judith. 'Good grief, what's got into you? Has it come to this? Yes, yes – I can see the evidence. The freshly turned soil. Incidentally, I can't get over the colour of the stuff you have in these parts – designer earth, some might call it. And your fingernails have rims to match.'

There seemed to be something amiss with Judith. She had phoned. 'Can I come over for lunch? I need a break.' She did not say from what, or why. Her manner now was a touch artificial. She talked with vigour and animation but her attention strayed. It was doing so at this moment. She sat on what passed for Stella's lawn, making a daisy chain and chewing her lip. The daisy chain broke and she threw it aside. 'I can't do this any more. You have to be about six. My fingers are too big.' She glanced up at Stella. 'Tell me . . . would you call yourself happy?'

'Of course not. I'm sixty-five. What is there to be happy about? Reasonably content, if you like. Most of the appetites still in good shape – bar one.'

'Oh, that . . .' said Judith. 'Why one ever made such a fuss about sex seems quite extraordinary now.'

Maybe I should enquire politely after Mary Binns, thought Stella. No – maybe not. It is perhaps from Mary Binns that Judith is taking a break.

'What happened to Dan Mitchell?' said Judith abruptly. 'I

mean – you don't see his name around in the papers any more . . .'

'Your train of association is disconcertingly direct, but never mind. He went to the States, a while ago. He worked there for Reuters. He had married an American lady.'

'Oh. I didn't know. I see.'

'My heart was not broken, if that's what you're discreetly not asking. It would never have worked out. By the time the American lady hove on the scene, we were exchanging the occasional postcard, that's all. I was even invited to the wedding.'

'Did you go?'

'Dear me, no. Old flames are spectres at the feast on such occasions. I wished them well and left it at that.'

This account perhaps begged questions and Judith was perhaps aware of this. 'To be honest,' she said, 'I can't remember him very well. You brought him to the dig once and another day we all had a picnic. That was about it. A funny time, that summer.'

'You can say that again.'

There was a silence. Both women revisited that other place, their other selves.

My turn, thought Stella. 'And Rosie?'

'Oh, Rosie . . . God! That's the first time I've even said her name in years. Mary once met up with a photo of her in my desk and . . . well, suffice it that Rosie became dangerous ground. I'd long since lost touch anyway. After Malta she got involved with a commune somewhere in Suffolk – remember communes? – and eventually drifted out of sight. But – oh, dear – we did have a nice time together . . . And now – wherever she may be – she's fifty-four. Year younger than me.

That I don't believe, frankly. Up here – ' Judith put her hands to her head – 'up here, in here, she's just as she was then. For ever will be.'

'Quite so,' said Stella. 'That's the saving grace, isn't it?'

'It's always knocked me sideways – the thought of what we carry around, stashed away. Not just what we know, but this business of stowing other people in the mind. I've always had an obsession with heads. Looking at people's heads. I can entirely understand the excitement the Victorians felt about phrenology. Burial excavations were always my favourite. That thrilling moment when you realize you've got the outline of a skull. I was dotty about skulls. Holding an entire skull. Looking into the eye sockets and thinking, inside there, once, were the answers to all the questions we'd like to ask . . .'

'You and Hamlet.'

'Don't be frivolous. I'm talking about a consuming passion. Some of my happiest hours have been spent putting together bits of cranium. Sherds always bored me stiff – the small change of archaeology, all those bloody pots. It was people I wanted to get my hands on. Reconstructing a cranium out of a heap of smashed bone.'

'Any chance of a dig?' Stella hardly liked to ask. Judith exuded discontent. Professional frustration was no doubt a large part of this.

Judith shook her head. 'And there are young turks coming on – they don't want the likes of me, even when there is something. Fair enough. I've had my turn, I suppose. But it doesn't come easy, kicking my heels day after day. I've been doing some copy-editing and proof reading for one of the trade publications, but that doesn't exactly stretch the mind.

I'm like a dog that's tied up – I've always needed to be out and about.'

'Too true,' said Stella. She associated Judith with movement, action, exterior scenes. Conversations in hired cars whipping through Italy and Greece; on foot in pursuit of remote Macedonian churches or belting around the cities of Europe. Those brief snatched holidays over the years: 'I could do a week in May – what about you?' Always with a charged itinerary – distances to be covered, unfrequented sites to be tracked down, elusive ruins to be notched up. As little time as possible to be spent under a roof. Even now, on a not especially warm day of early summer, they were out here – a rug spread on the damp grass – because Judith didn't want to be cooped up inside.

She sprawled there in jeans and a sweatshirt. Adolescent dress. An adolescent outline, too, from the rear – thin bony backside, dark cropped cap of hair. Only when she turned her head did you see the years. The decades engraved there in texture of skin, the set of lips, the fold of an eyelid.

'I don't resent getting older.' Judith rolled on to her back and stared up at Stella. 'Most of the bones I've dug up kicked the bucket long before my age now. Three score years and ten is a lot of nonsense – there weren't many in biblical times who got to that. We have a pretty good run for our money these days. It's not ageing and it's not the banking of the fires and all that. It's being put out to grass. Sidelined when you've still got plenty of mileage left. Don't you feel that?'

'I'm ten years older, remember. But yes – quite often I do.'

'We're in the wrong business. Politics is the thing, if you play your cards right. Prime ministers and presidents totter on into their seventies. Always have done. Old bones are likely to have been powerful bones – that was a good excavation rule of thumb.'

'I thought it was more a case of "Uneasy lies the head that wears a crown . . ."'

'You've got Shakespeare on the brain today. He's not infallible. He coined truisms to suit circumstances. And he didn't know anything about demographic history. Right?' Judith cocks an eyebrow at Stella, grins.

'No one did, until recently. He based his statistics on the life expectancy of medieval rulers, presumably.'

'Where better than average living circumstances had to be offset against the risks of assassination or death in combat. Always the problem, for the aristocracy. But physique wins out – more protein – larger, stronger, longer-lived people. The case here, until recently. Tory members of Parliament were several inches taller than Labour members, on average.' Judith sat up abruptly. 'However did we get on to this? But you've perked me up. Served up some distraction. I don't feel quite so glum. I'd better be off now, though, or . . .'

Or what? thought Stella later. Or Mary Binns will be asking questions, probably. How did Judith get herself into *that*? The same way, of course, that any of us fetch up with someone else – that combination of happenstance, passion, opportunity, inertia . . . The same way others of us fetch up alone, for better or for worse.

For better, she felt at that moment, recalling Judith's restless state. Pedigree Chum for supper, she said to the dog. Chicken flavour. And maybe an evening walk, if you're good.

Chapter Eleven

'It's not ageing and it's not the banking of the fires . . .' But age and ageing are a matter of absolute confusion, Stella reflected. An anarchic situation, a Lewis Carroll state in which, like Alice, you do not know where or who you are at all. Passports and other documents made these prescriptive statements, but the reality is quite different. The reality has an eerie affinity with childhood, which is a continuous present. One moves obediently from day to day, but carrying this freight of reference that sends one flying in all directions, let loose in time and space, both then and there at the same time as one is now and here.

The various papers in Stella's desk told her that she was sixty-five. The face in the mirror – at which she gave only the most perfunctory glances these days – seemed like some disturbing distortion of her real face. These jowls, those pouches. The backs of her hands were brocaded with brown blotches beneath which twined the thick grey worms of veins. But miraculously preserved within this uncompromising prison of flesh and bone were all those other Stellas, all co-existing, all bearing witness, all available for consultation. Tell me how it was, she could say to some vanished Stella, and back would come these accounts of elsewhere and other people. The Delta, Orkney, Malta. Nadine, Don, Alan Scarth.

All present and correct. The invisible universe to which each of us has access.

In dreams Stella revisited all these other incarnations of herself. She was never Stella now but some free-floating, ageless, unconstrained Stella for whom all options remained open. Like a child, she accepted without question the circumstances in which she found herself. Babies might turn into pigs, pigs might fly, clouds become loaves of bread. She dreamed of sex and love with vivid strangers. She moved through bizarre landscapes which melted one into another like the chessboard squares beyond the looking glass and then she awoke to the relentless solidity of the real world, astonished at the ingenuities of the subconscious.

She woke also to a reality that continued to surprise her – this house that was apparently hers, this pleasant landscape in which she had fortuitously arrived with her little cargo of tangible possessions and that huge invisible ballast to which she made continuous private reference. She was comfortable enough with these surroundings, but still not certain how she had got here or why. In the past there had been good reason to be wherever she found herself. Now, she was where she was simply because one had to be somewhere.

And in the past there had been work. Each day sprang up to meet her with its agenda of goals and obligations. There were mountainous days and days when the going looked good, daunting days and days that induced a glow of anticipation. Now, days stretched ahead undemanding and indistinguishable – a bland flat track marching into the distance. Come along, they said. Go ahead. What's the problem?

The problem was this unchallenging vista, Stella realized. If you are conditioned by a lifetime of endeavour, then lack of direction is unnerving. And thus it was that the letter from the editor of an anthropological journal came as a welcome prompt. The editor – a former colleague – reminded Stella of her promise to supply an article and hoped – sardonically? prophetically? – that she was now sufficiently settled and restored to contemplate a mild professional work-out. Wonderful if you could. Five thousand words for the winter number?

The article was to be a personal perspective on the issue of gender in field work. The gender of the ethnographer, of course – the gender issues of those under study were another matter and already discussed into the ground, over decades. Stella was to consider her own experience in the field and examine the implications of being a woman, with the wisdom of hindsight and comparisons of her reception by different cultures and communities. She was to record her own problems in relation to such questions as conformity, reciprocity and culture shock, and discuss how her own attitudes and methods of adjustment had altered over the years. She was to take a long view. She was to consider herself a guru, a pundit.

Be personal, said the editor. Most of our stuff is so dry. Inevitably, but even so . . . Give us a shot in the arm.

And so, pleasurably propelled into activity, Stella set to. She cleared her desk, located a wodge of A4 typing paper and unpacked her old portable electronic typewriter from the box in which it had sat since her arrival in the cottage. She had been a competent enough user of departmental computers, but saw no reason to spend money now on one of her own. Besides, the neat little machine reminded her of its ancestral predecessors, the Remington manuals on which she had tapped away in the Delta, in Malta . . .

I shall get stuck in all this week, she told herself. And the next. And quite possibly the one after. Batten down the hatches. Air the dog before breakfast and dinner. Switch the phone off.

Message 1 on Stella's answering machine
Hi! It's me – Judith. You're tramping the moor, I suppose. Or throwing sticks on the beach for that ridiculous animal. Don't bother to ring back – I'm going away for a few days. I'm not calling about anything special, just . . . Anyway . . . maybe I'll write. Take care.

Stella assembles notebooks and card indexes. She pores over these. Sometimes she pores for hours. She reads, intent, and then she stares out of the window. Sometimes she stares for long periods.

The dog watches Stella. If she looks in his direction, he wags his tail in frantic appeal. Once in a while, when things get too much, he hurls himself against her knees.

Message 2 on Stella's answering machine
Richard speaking – Richard Faraday. I'm sorry to have missed you. Please don't trouble to return the call – merely one or two thoughts I've had that might be useful to you. I'll try another time. I trust all goes well. Goodbye for now.

Stella takes a pad and pen and starts to rough out a structure for this article. She will move from the general to the particular. She will look at the problems which confront all ethnographers in the field, discuss those which challenge women in particular, and move from there to an account and consideration of her own experience. She will make what deductions are possible from this and return for her conclusion to a general survey of the implications.

Straightforward enough, you would think.

Straightforward enough. A doddle. An agreeable, time-consuming doddle. Except that somehow it is not. This effortless glide from the general to the particular is more easily proposed than done. In fact, when push comes to shove, it seems that it cannot be done at all. The general is no problem. She can still witter on with the best of them, she discovers – hold forth about cross-cultural modes and defensive behaviours and variant roles. But when it comes to the particular . . . Well, the particular simply rises up with such clarity and vigour that there is no way of reducing it to words. Reaching out and pinning it down in neat typed sequences on the white page in front of her.

Stella stares out of the window at the particular.

From time to time what she sees is overridden by intrusive external images. A tractor grinds past. The Hiscox boys ride by on rusting push-bikes. Some while later the red car hurtles along the lane, too fast as usual. Just now, Stella is not interested in any of these phenomena.

Their mother was waiting for them. 'Where've you been, then?'

They mumbled something. The village. Get a Coke.

'You've been longer than it takes to get a Coke.'

Michael's bike. Stupid bloody bike. Chain come off and we had to fix it. If we had proper bikes.

And she's off, of course. 'D'you know what a new bike costs? And where do you think the money's coming from?

Mountain bikes, you've got in mind, I dare say. A thousand quid. D'you think we work ourselves into the ground to get you shiny new toys?'

And so on. Hands on hips, bawling at them. 'Where d'you think you're off to now? I'm talking to you. You'll go when I say so, got that?'

The day before, she'd caught them smoking. They were behind the sheds and suddenly she was there, too. Peter dropped his fag but Michael was too late – his was still in his hand.

She stepped forward and clipped his hand, swiped so hard the cigarette flew up and away. His hand stung. The cigarette landed in a patch of dry grass. A grass stem flared up and then lay there smouldering. The boys stared at it – the yellow flame, the little coil of smoke.

'Next time I catch you, your father'll give you something to worry about. Got that?'

Something boiled over. Michael said, 'Why shouldn't I fucking well smoke?'

A mistake. She told him. She told them out there for ten minutes and more, shouting away. 'Because I say so, that's why. Because I'm your mother and I say so and that's all you need to know, so get that clear in your head for starters . . .' And she went on telling them for the rest of the day, every time she set eyes on them, every time they couldn't manage to get away from her.

They went and banged at the corrugated iron. The shed. This shed they were making. They hit the metal till it bounced, till the noise rang in their ears. Bang, bang, bang. She thinks she's got everyone on the run, they told each other, she thinks she's top dog, but she doesn't know everything. There's things she fucking doesn't know, aren't there, and fucking never will know, will she? Bang, bang, bang.

They told each other, too, that the old woman in the cottage was staring at them when they went past. Staring out of the window at them. Thinking what stupid rotten bikes they'd got. Ignorant old cow. She better not watch them like that or they'd sort her out.

Stella thinks about Dina, in the Delta village. Dina, who was also a woman, but a woman with very different expectations and assumptions. She wonders how to draw upon her relationship with Dina to inform this article. Her relationships with Dina and with Dina's sisters and mother, and with Saleh and with the neighbours and indeed everyone else. She toys with words and sentences – 'The villagers' perception of me as a woman . . . my sex conditioned male responses to the extent that . . . where the gender issue arose in my transactions with other women . . .' – but the stern language immediately dissolves and is replaced by something much more pertinent. A specific problem which confronts the female ethnographer.

The female ethnographer must take with her into the field sufficient sanitary requisites for the duration of the field trip.

'What is this?' enquires Dina, who likes to inspect Stella's belongings from time to time. She indicates the four-month supply of Tampax. Dina is accompanied by her sister, her sister-in-law and her twelve-year-old niece.

Stella draws a breath and explains.

The women listen in amazement. The niece claps both hands over her mouth, aghast.

'Up inside there?' says Dina, in disbelief. There is an outbreak of shocked whispering and muttering. Stella cannot follow what is being said, until at last Dina enlightens her. She points out – none too delicately – that if and when – *inshallah!* – Stella eventually finds herself a husband, she will not be able to convince him of her virginity. She will not be intact.

'Ah . . .' says Stella. 'Well . . . Mmn . . . I see what you mean.'

Be personal, said the editor. How personal?

'Nice view you must have out of that window,' says the postman. 'Seen you sitting there every morning this week. And last week. Nothing for you yesterday, but there's a couple today. The electricity, you won't thank me for that, but the other's got a foreign stamp. We're due rain this afternoon, they're saying, and if you're thinking of going to Minehead, don't, the A39's jammed solid in both directions.'

Letter from Judith to Stella

I'm in Crete – a cheapo package hol. Sudden rush of blood to the head. I can't afford it, but what the hell. I felt desperate to be somewhere sunny and ancient. Mary not too pleased – she's tied down at work so couldn't have come anyway (I've a feeling she suspects I've sneaked off with you). I've hired a scooter and spend my time nosing around Minoan sites. Everyone else sits on the beach toasting their skin cancer. How does your garden grow? That was a good afternoon we spent nattering on your lawn, by the way – sorry I was a bit glum. But you did me a power of good. You always have. Probably you've never realized that. Like I bet you never knew I carried a tremendous torch for you once. Years back. Post Rosie. Luckily I had more sense than to let on. And don't worry – I got over it long ago. Hey – that sounds rather rude, now I come to think of it. But you know what I mean . . . The hotel is a concrete blockhouse. The company is vile. No matter

– I found a couple of Minoan sherds in the car-park and I've wallowed in the Herakleon museum and sat in the dust under olive trees and pretended I was taking time off from a dig . . .

Stella considers what women have in common. She tries to see where cultural difference ends and collective experience begins.

Bodies. Having this body rather than a male body. Breasts, vagina. Being equipped for parturition.

And?

Certain tendencies, we are told. A greater capacity for empathy, for intuition.

Certain deficiencies also, in some cases. A distinct lack of mechanical skills. An inability to change a wheel.

Stella squats in the dust beside the Renault – the elderly, capricious, accursed Renault – and wrestles with the jack. Adroit changing of a wheel does not require a great degree of physical strength, she perceives, so there is no reason why she (or indeed any other woman) should not be able to do it with perfect success. But it is a matter of getting on equal terms with nuts and spanners and this blasted metal contraption which slips and wobbles and will not do what she can see it is intended to do.

And all the while Manolo watches her. Manolo is the next-door neighbour of Despina, the widow from whom Stella rents the room over the coffee shop. Manolo and Despina do not get on. Manolo is the wide boy of the Greek village, an agreeable rogue who earns a living as a Jack-of-all-trades in this place where most people are peasant farmers.

Manolo strolls across the road. 'I will do it for you.'

Stella is now nicely wrong-footed. Her control of personal circumstances is in question and Manolo has his own agenda, as she well knows. Manolo will demand a quid pro quo by way of lifts to neighbouring villages. Stella's is one of only three cars in the village and she has had to make a firm rule that she will only act as a taxi in cases of emergency. If her landlady, in particular, were to see Manolo in the passenger seat of the Renault, there would be considerable ill feeling. But Stella is sorely tempted to accept the offer. She has been at this for over half an hour now and she has better things to do.

She sits back to draw breath. She remembers Despina, whirring deftly at the treadle sewing machine on which she does business as the village seamstress. Stella has watched Despina with respect, knowing that she herself could not even begin to do what she does with such panache. Maybe mechanical aptitude is not entirely a matter of gender.

Manolo slides the jack under the Renault. There is a clunk and a click. He has it in place. He starts to crank it up. He suggests that maybe he should also change the oil. This is not a job for a woman, he says kindly. He will be very happy to see to the car for her. It is no trouble, no trouble at all.

Stella is defeated. By Manolo's opportunism. By the diabolical Renault. By her own technical incompetence. She glares at man and car.

Stella tries to nail the salient issues – the points at which gender defines the position of the woman ethnographer. The trouble is that she finds that frequently she is thinking simply about being a woman. The woman and the woman ethnographer keep fusing, as of course they did back then, out there.

Manolo's dark Byzantine gaze was often distinctly lubricious, she remembers. She could read in it exactly what he thought about her as a woman. Manolo, accordingly, had to be kept at arm's length, along with others of the younger village men. Her dealings with them were tempered with more caution than her dealings with the women. With the women there is some elemental bond, despite the yawning difference in their circumstances.

She hunts for language – for a way in which to turn the pageant in her head into sober reflective professional sentences.

The red car speeds past the window again. Stella thinks briefly of Karen Hiscox. Elemental bond?

'This one's mine,' said Michael.

They liked killing rabbits. She'd shouted at them out of the car window as she was going: 'And you can do me three rabbits before I get back. Kill and skin. Got that?'

Skinning was a bind but killing they enjoyed, and they'd never let on to her that they did. If she knew they liked something, then they only got to do it when it suited her.

The way they jerk and then go limp at once if you've made a proper job of it. It gave them a feeling of being in control, on top of things. Same as shooting. Lining up a pigeon and seeing it drop. They'd only done that a few times, in fact. Their father hardly ever let them have a go with the gun – just once in a while if he was in a good mood or if she thought it was worth having a few pigeons to sell. Sometimes when they knew they were on their own, they'd go and handle the gun, just to get the feel of it – practise lining up the sights, looking along the barrel, imagining the bird or the animal moving about, with no idea of what was coming to it and then . . . wham!

Card from Richard Faraday to Stella

My phone calls fall on stony ground – I take it you must be away. This is to await your return and is merely to say that I know a garage that is both obliging and reasonable – you mentioned a problem with your car. Also, I can warmly recommend the coastal walk from Porlock to Culbone, if you have not tried it. On a more personal note, I am conscious of having been perhaps a touch ambivalent during our dinner together about Nadine's feelings towards you. Nadine greatly admired you. Possibly this may never have been apparent – she had a way of camouflaging her responses. Nevertheless, you became something of an icon – despite the divergence of the ways. Your work. Your personality.

Perhaps we could meet up for a meal before too long. I got the impression that restaurant is not perhaps quite to your taste. There is an agreeable pub in Luxborough.

Yours,

Richard

Stella has not lost sight of the issue of gender in field-work. She is confronting it head on, indeed. She has considered a selection of particular instances where gender could be said to have muddied the waters – she will have to think of a more elegant phrase for purposes of the article. She now looks out of the window, through the contemporary veil of green summer Somerset and contemplates a scene in which her sex was indeed the driving force. This scene is a personal possession and not relevant to the article but she reviews it none the less, with complicated feelings.

'Who did your mother's youngest sister marry?' she asks. She looks at him with calm neutrality, wearing an expression of professional enquiry, her pen poised.

'Nobody,' says Alan. 'She was obstinate and awkward, like yourself, and she thought she knew best, even though she had the finest men in Orkney at her feet. She ended up a sour old maid in a bungalow outside Kirkwall.'

Stella consults her notes. 'Alan Scarth,' she says, 'your aunt Annie married a Rendell, had three children and is farming yet on Westray.'

'Then why are you needing to ask me?'

'A degree of cross-checking is advisable in field-work,' says Stella. 'I've left you till last, you know. Everyone else I've done – man, woman and child – except for old Richie, who's really not up to it.'

'I'm well aware of that,' he says. 'Left out, I've felt. Excluded. Now my uncle Ben, I can tell you about. He married an incomer. A beautiful woman with red hair she was. She came from the south one summer and he knew at once she was the one for him. And she knew it, too, though it took him a while to persuade her. Married in the autumn they were, and a grand life they had together.'

Stella looks at her notes again. 'You don't have any uncles, Alan.'

'True enough,' says he. And he gazes at her across the table, over the yellow checked oilcloth, which is cracked and worn so that the squares leach into one another. Outside the window a curlew calls, and then an oyster-catcher.

Stella sighs. She puts down her pen. 'Alan,' she says. 'Why should you be the only person on the island apparently unable or unwilling to co-operate in the completion of a simple questionnaire on lineage structures?'

'You know why,' he says. 'You know why very well, Miss Stella Brentwood.'

So does it all boil down to physique, thinks Stella. Bodies. The bodies of women, which are so crucially equipped. Which are emblematic. And she remembers suddenly the votive figures found at Maltese neolithic sites – crude fertility goddesses with bulbous stomachs, pendulous breasts, vast thighs and tiny faceless heads. Celebrations of reproductive power, presumably, or propitiatory offerings. Whatever they were, they were awesome, loaded still with some primeval significance. She had asked Judith what they meant and Judith had laughed. 'Well, it's pretty obvious, isn't it? The sex bombs, we call them.'

Their descendants still reigned, the matriarchs who sat outside their houses, monitoring the village, the rippling flesh of their vast bodies majestically shrouded in black.

North Somerset Herald

Kingston Florey Mothers' Union

Members met at Wisteria Cottage. Owing to the unavoidable absence of the expected speaker, a DIY meeting was held with a wide-ranging discussion on matters of common interest. Mrs Walters won the raffle, and the competition for the best craft item for a bazaar was won by Mrs Selwood with a striking nude female figurine carved from Watchet Alabaster.

Minehead Ladies Bowls

Minehead sent three rinks to Wellington but on an enjoyable afternoon the home side proved too strong for the visitors. Minehead gained maximum points when they played Ilminster in the South and West Somerset League and won home and away and overall by 10 shots.

Porlock played five rinks of triples in the Exmoor Trophy League against Minehead and won by 14 shots.

Arson Suspected

Minehead Fire Brigade were called out to a barn fire at Little Mayton farm near Kingston Florey last Wednesday. Twenty bales of hay were lost before the blaze was extinguished. The police are pursuing inquiries.

Chapter Twelve

Departure from the cottage by car was always a serious undertaking. The car had to be backed out of the standing space into the lane in such a way that you did not clip the corner of the hedge. Preoccupied by this delicate manoeuvre, Stella did not hear the throb of a tractor until she was safely out and saw in her mirror that Ted Hiscox loomed above the car in his red monster, impassively waiting for her to move on. Her gesture of apology was met with a nod of acceptance. But now she had stalled the engine. And it would not re-start. Battery a bit low, maybe. She turned the key again, and again. That obstinate dying whirr each time. Damn. And now, for heaven's sake, here was John Morgan grinding towards her from the opposite direction, so she was entirely trapped with everything soaring up around her – hedgebanks, trees and the two towering machines between which she was sandwiched.

She tried the engine again. Whirr . . . Ah, but it caught then – a promising little cough. The two men gazed down at her from the shuddering tractors.

Whirr . . . cough. Whirr . . . cough. She wound down her window and bawled in the direction of John Morgan, 'Sorry – I seem to have a problem.'

Not to worry, said the wave of his hand. Take your time.

But the sense of significant labour inconveniently suspended hung in the air, increasing Stella's embarrassment.

She turned the key again. Triumph, at last. She revved the engine, gave a thumbs up. But now John Morgan must reverse before she could continue, and did so with practised skill, roaring backwards into the nearest passing place. Stella beamed a smile of humiliation and apology.

Unnerved, she turned the wrong way on to the main road, forgetting her destination. It was several minutes before she remembered that she was going to lunch with Richard Faraday and should be heading in the opposite direction. She took a detour to loop back on to the road, thinking of this small incident in the lane. One which nicely defined her, she saw, as a passing obstruction to the real business of this place.

She had spent much time, over the years, watching people work – in the process of working herself, though no doubt it did not look like that to the objects of her interest. This odd foreign woman forever hanging around, asking questions. And the work she watched had been for the most part a communal affair, filled with human exchange. People calling to each other across fields, or from the back of a donkey. Those Orkney tractors had no excluding driver cabs – you rode exposed to the elements, and to anyone you chanced to meet. The grainy photographs in booklets about west Somerset in earlier times showed a world of collective labour – a dozen men hay-making, a whole group attending to a threshing-machine, gangs of miners by the mineral line, the crowded attendance at the village smithy.

Those you worked with were also those to whom you were related and you probably lived along the road from them, too. None of this solitude and self-sufficiency. Indeed, plunging off the main road presently into unfamiliar territory in search of Richard's place, she noted the emptiness of the landscape and thought again of those teeming Delta fields and the old Somerset photographs.

Richard was standing at the gate.

'I got lost. But I'm not *that* late.'

'My fault – I must have neglected to send you a copy of my location map.'

'You sent it,' said Stella cheerfully. 'I forgot it. Anyway, it gave me a chance to explore your patch. Very nice too.'

A scatter of colour-washed cottages in a cup of pitching fields and woodland. A stream running alongside the road, with little bridges across it. A small ancient-looking chapel of perfect simplicity perched above a hedgebank that sparkled with flowers. Sometimes it was difficult to take this landscape seriously – to remember that it had evolved from centuries of agricultural endeavour and blithe environmental disregard. At points it could look like a carefully designed scenic effect, probably for the sort of calendar pressed upon customers by local garages.

'Well, it suits me,' said Richard crisply. 'The fruit of many months of careful search.'

The house was that desired combination of old and new. A former farmhouse prinked and polished. Clean. Ordered. Squashy sofa. Shining tables. Flowers in a cut-glass vase.

And Nadine. Stella had forgotten that Nadine would be there. On Richard's desk, framed in her wedding dress. Laughing, on the mantelpiece, with a small child in her arms.

There in that patchwork cushion on the armchair. A scrap of material on which glows a cluster of scarlet cherries. Nadine's cherry dress, for heaven's sake . . .

*

149

They sail down the Broad. Nadine is wearing her cherry dress because she is in pursuit of a man and the cherry dress is her most becoming garment, with its nipped-in waist, tight bust and sweetheart neckline, all of which make the most of her nubile figure. She is also shivering, because the cherry dress is cotton and has short sleeves. This is the beginning of what is known as the Summer Term, but May in Oxford is frequently chill. Stella is more appropriately wearing a jersey and skirt. She has been hauled out of the library because Nadine needs an accomplice for this venture. They are going to the Kemp, where the man on whom Nadine has currently set her sights will almost certainly be having coffee with a group of friends. Nadine has made herself *au fait* with his habits. They will drift into the Kemp, locate the target, drift past his table and, with any luck, be invited to join the party.

Nadine rubs her goose-flesh. 'What we do for love . . .'

Stella has been reading about Eleanor of Aquitaine, a powerful woman who bucked the trend of her day. The role of women is not much addressed in the Oxford history syllabus of the fifties, and Stella's consideration of Eleanor of Aquitaine has prompted various thoughts. She sees that Eleanor is clever and shrewd, which helps, but that in the last resort her principal weapon was sex. On whom would it be most expedient to bestow her body? But this visible woman has made her think also of all those women who are historically invisible. She has been thinking about gender, equally out of step with her times, for the matter is by no means a burning issue, though beginning perhaps to simmer gently. The presence of Stella, Nadine and a few hundred other women in this ancient bastion of male privilege is of course a crucial element in the simmering process, though few of them yet think of it thus.

Least of all, at the moment, Nadine. 'I'm going to get him to take me to Magdalen Commem,' she says. 'Or bust.'

'Then prepare to bust,' says Stella. 'Susan Lamming is after him too.'

'I can see off Susan Lamming.'

They pause in the entrance of Blackwell's for Nadine to whip out a mirror and check her appearance.

'Isn't it odd?' says Stella. 'Here we are, theoretically stuck into the Wars of the Roses and Rousseau, and most of the time we're thinking about sex.'

Nadine corrects her. 'Men. Specific men.'

'Same thing.'

'Not entirely. There's what's to happen in the long run. One is getting in some practice. Marriage. I intend to get married when I'm twenty-three.'

'Is that what you're going to say to John Hobhouse in the Kemp?'

Nadine giggles. 'Don't be an idiot. Magdalen Commem is all that matters at the moment.' She adjusts the bodice of the cherry dress, twitches the skirt. 'Come on.'

They climb the stairs to the coffee shop. The room is a jabbering mass of undergraduates, peppered with a few stoical Oxford citizens, all of them obscured by a blue haze of cigarette smoke. Nadine pauses, searches, identifies the target. 'There ... over in the far corner. You go in front. Look conspicuous.'

They weave their way through the tables, *Vénus tout entière* ...

'I thought we might eat outside,' said Richard. He led Stella through French windows on to a paved area overlooking a garden as manicured as the house. The paved area was skirted by ornamental pots brimming with flowers that Stella could not identify. A table was laid and chairs drawn up.

'Admire my garden while I bring things out.' He vanished and Stella admired, or, rather, decided that this paved bit could only be called a patio, that the farmhouse was indeed well and truly deracinated, and that she rather liked this plant with cascading pink flowers.

Richard returned carrying a tray. Some cold salmon. Potato salad. A green salad. A bottle of Chardonnay in a wine cooler.

'You have the advantage of me,' said Stella. 'I'm no gardener, I have discovered. What's that pink thing called?'

'Diascia. I have a spare, if you'd like one.'

'No. I'd kill it. I seem to be some sort of sport. Horticulture is traditionally women's work, the world over. Not in my case. I am the kiss of death, it seems. Never mind, I quite enjoy the slash and burn aspect.'

'You are not unique. Nadine was only a dilettante gardener. I have come to it late and do it with method and application because that is the sort of person I am. Trained thus. Give me a brief and I master it.' He finished arranging the food and sat down. 'You have been very unobtainable. Were you away?'

'Actually, I have been doing some work.' Stella outlined her article.

'I'd like to read it at some point if I may.'

'By all means.'

Richard began to describe a walk he had taken across the moor. Yes, Stella thought, he is a man who deals with what comes his way, whatever it is. Civil Service tasks. Family life. Retirement. He would get on and make a good job of it.

Grimly, perhaps, but he'd buckle to. No pointless keening when the fates turn nasty. Nadine's death. No raking over the ashes and staring out of windows. Roll the lawn. Plant out the pink things. Diascias.

'When I feel particularly lonely,' said Richard, 'a long walk is strangely therapeutic. Dear me – I forgot to give us any napkins. Excuse me . . .'

She stared after him, startled. Chastened, even. Never think that surface appearance is the whole story. To tell the truth, she thought, I have never taken much notice of him. Nadine's husband, simply. She realized that she could barely remember the first time she met him. Nadine saying, 'This is Richard.' A shadowy figure with whom she had exchanged silent inspection which confirmed that neither was much interested in the other. After that, the token friendship of those united by a third person.

Richard returned and resumed eating. 'So what is the difference between men and women – did you come to any conclusion? Men and women anthropologists, that is to say.'

'Much the same things as in real life, I eventually decided. Women are more easily defeated by machinery. Which is why you have this green sward and I do not. The lawnmower splutters and dies as soon as I touch it. On the other hand, women relate to one another, the world over. Possibly more readily than men do.'

'If you would like me to come and deal with the lawnmower, please let me know. I take your point about women relating. I used to envy Nadine that capacity. Her friendships were always more effortless than mine. But that may have been a personal failing. Many men are distinctly tribal – in a gender sense.'

'Of course,' said Stella. 'You see it in action on all sides.

From football terraces to warrior dances. But that's *doing*. It's other kinds of empathy I had in mind. Feelings. Responses.'

'The football fan would no doubt claim he is feeling and responding. Warriors, too, I fear. Have you had professional dealings with any of these?'

'No. My area was rather tamer. Lineage and kinship. Community life.'

A pall of grey cloud which had tilted across the sky while they were eating now began to spit warm rain. Stella helped Richard to move the remains of the meal into the kitchen and then wandered into the sitting-room while he made coffee. She stood in front of the bookcase, searching for a work on local history that he had mentioned. Sets of the classics. Poetry. Prominent biographies of recent years. A scatter of contemporary fiction. A shelf of history with, tucked away at the end, the familiar dark-blue, gold-lettered spines of the volumes of *The Oxford History of England*. Nadine's, of course. Just as I still have mine, thought Stella. But we alternated volumes. Swopped. She never had Collingwood & Myres. I never had Stenton. 'Can I borrow your *Anglo-Saxon England*?'

'It's all very well for you,' wails Nadine. 'You've worked. I haven't. This is where I get found out. It's like dying and discovering God exists after all and there He is at the gates of Heaven saying, No, not you, scram, you didn't believe in Me.'

'It would be St Peter,' says Stella. 'It's he who does turnstile duty.'

It is early on a fine May morning. They are part of a sombre stream of black-clad youth heading for the Examination Schools. Although, on closer inspection, the sobriety of dress is nicely manipulated, not least by Nadine and Stella. The regulations state merely that subfusc apparel for examination wear must be black and white. Men wear black suits and white shirts. Nadine wears a full black skirt, wide belt to accentuate the waist and frothy white nylon blouse at the neck of which is the required black tie – a great pussy-cat bow of black taffeta. Stella wears a black pencil skirt which is as short as she dares, exposing a lot of fetching leg in black nylons. Her shirt is crisp white piqué, her tie a shoestring velvet ribbon.

'Trust you to know that,' says Nadine. 'You know your Stubbs Charters too, don't you? And your Civil War and your Industrial Revolution and your Slavery and Secession and your European History Part Two.'

'Only up to a point.'

'You'll get a First, blast you. I feel sick. Maybe I'll just faint when I see the paper. Do you get an aegrotat if you faint?'

'I don't think so.'

'Perhaps it'll be that heavenly man from Christ Church invigilating. I went to all his lectures just to look at him. Hang on a minute, your seams are crooked.'

They step into the porch of St Mary's to make adjustments to their stockings. 'I've even got a black suspender belt on,' says Nadine. 'I thought it might bring me luck. And don't tell me luck doesn't come into it. This is the worst moment of my life, it's worth trying anything.'

They complete the last few hundred yards. They climb the steps of the fateful building. They search for their names on the list. The seating is in alphabetical order; they will not be in the same room. Nadine rolls her eyes, clutches Stella's arm for a moment and is swallowed by the crowd.

Sitting at her desk, Stella sees that she is surrounded by

men. One or two are acquaintances, others she knows by sight. All they have in common is that their surname begins with B and they have been exposed to the same information for the last three years. Men outnumber women by ten to one. However, it is not this fact that engages her attention but a strange detached perception of the whole scene, as though she were no longer a participant. She sees it suddenly as a ritual, entirely baffling to anyone who did not know what was going on (thus perhaps is the anthropologist born). It is as though she rises and floats up to the top of the great room with its high windows and stares down at this ceremonially clad throng of initiates. The ranks of desks, the bent heads, the sense of portent. The priestly figure who walks between the rows, bestowing sheets of printed paper. The small defiant gestures – the men who wear a buttonhole, a carnation or a rose, the girls with their manipulations of the dress code. The scene becomes ripe for exegesis and deconstruction, like some inscrutable practice of another age. What are these people about to do? Why are there so many men and so few women? What is the significance of their apparel, their silence, their air of resignation?

One day, she thinks, I shall look back at this moment and it will be neither here nor there. Except that it will, because what sort of degree I get may well decide which way I go next.

'Ah,' said Richard. 'You're looking for the book on the mineral line.'

'I was. But then I started thinking about Schools. That traumatic business. Did you know that Nadine wore a black suspender belt, for luck?'

'No, but it sounds entirely in character. Though I fear it

didn't help. She got a Third, whereas you of course got the anticipated First. Not that she held it against you – she saw both results as perfectly appropriate.'

And so that time is inextricably wound into everything that has happened to me since, thought Stella. The First meant I could go ahead and do the diploma and thus I ended up as I have. Hence the rest of life, or at least the framework thereof.

Richard had by now found the required book. 'Here we are. Borrow it.'

'Thank you. It's a daunting thought – the way in which your fate is largely fixed by what happens to you when barely out of adolescence.'

'Do you feel that yours went awry, then?'

'Certainly not,' said Stella. 'I meant simply that you point in a particular direction when still in a state of confusion.' It occurred to her as she spoke that Richard was a man who had very likely never been in such a condition. But does anyone decide to become a civil servant at the age of twenty? Well, yes – plenty do, or the country would have long since ground to a halt.

'Black coffee or white?' said Richard. 'What I really wanted to be was an opera singer.'

'Black, please.' So there you go – civil servant is *faute de mieux*, as is right and proper.

'But the Bach Choir was as far as I ever got in that direction. A run-of-the-mill tenor, that's all I was.'

It occurred to Stella as they talked that Nadine had referred little to her husband, over the years. Seminal events, from time to time – a promotion, some professional *coup*. The children got more of a showing. The impression given of Richard was that of an essential backdrop. What he said or thought was not part of Nadine's periodic accounts of family life. The letters and cards. Those occasions, decreasing over the years, when she and Stella met for a meal or an outing. Richard was simply there, one understood, a crucial continuity, the basic accessory to the life that Nadine had always planned. And Stella herself had come to think of him thus. Or, rather, had barely thought of him at all. No wonder, then, that he now proved occasionally unpredictable.

He stood at the window of her car as she was leaving. 'Bear in mind my offer to sort out your recalcitrant machine.'

No, she thought as she drove away, I can't sink so low. That it should come to this – Nadine's husband offering to mend my lawnmower.

When she turned off the main road into the lane she saw in the distance that the Hiscox boys were loitering outside the cottage, wheeling bicycles. Up to some mischief while she had been gone? She speeded up, suspicious, and they at once rode off in the direction of the bungalow. Back at the cottage, she made a tour of inspection but could find nothing amiss. Everything seemed normal, Bracken ecstatic in welcome.

The old woman's car wasn't there so the boys went round the back of the cottage and rattled on the windows a bit to start the stupid dog barking. They nosed around for a while and then they came back round the cottage on to the lane – dog barking and barking still – and the woman's car was turning in off the main road so they pushed off back home.

Chapter Thirteen

She was waiting on the doorstep when they got back from school. Hands on her hips. That look on her face. 'So where've you been?'

School bus was late.

'The school bus wasn't late. I phoned. I wasn't born yesterday. I've been on to the school and the bus left dead on time. And you're twenty minutes late. So where've you been, I'd like to know? You've been off somewhere buying cigarettes, haven't you? Right, then, that's no cash for either of you for as long as I decide and don't bother to ask how long that's going to be . . .'

And so on. She'd got it in for them, for days and days now, not letting up. It had begun with catching them smoking and then them saying that about needing new bikes and now she was on a roll, letting rip half a dozen times a day, jumping on them as soon as they were back from school. But she was letting their father have it too, just as much. Winding him up till he burst out and then sticking her fingers in her ears. 'Can't hear a word you're saying. I'm not interested. Tra-la, tra-la, tra-la.'

You'd have thought they could get together – the two of them and their father. But it didn't work that way. Their father just boxed himself off when things were like this. Didn't open his mouth. Slammed out of the house and worked in the sheds. You did best to keep away from him.

At meal times she banged food down in front of them. Things she knew they didn't like. Disgusting fish. Muck worse than school dinners. She didn't eat it herself. Maybe she didn't eat. Maybe it was something else that kept her going – kept her revved up like that. Not drink, though, nor smoking. Something inside her, it was. Something that gave her a charge.

Something that made her not like anyone else. Mad, they'd heard someone say once. That woman's mad. They hadn't been supposed to hear.

They'd talked about this, afterwards. But she couldn't be mad, because mad people can't cope, can they? Gran was mad, pretty well, because she didn't know her own name half the time and forgot anything she was told. Their mother could cope all right. She coped everyone else into the ground. She coped them out of her way.

That was how to get on top, no question. You had to sort people out before they had time to mess you up, like she did. They'd watched her to see how it was done, they'd been watching her at it since before they could remember. They'd tried it, too. At school. And it worked – people left them alone. They didn't have any mates, but they didn't care about that. Nor did she, and she didn't care either. I don't give a damn about anyone, she'd say – got that?

So nor did they. Except for her. They hated her but she was the only person they wanted to please. They felt as though they were split in half. Often they wanted to kill her, always they'd do anything – bloody anything – to have her take notice of them, be in a good mood with them.

When there was no chance of that, like now, they went around looking for something to smash up.

Hi! says Judith. I'm back. Been back for some while, in fact, but I couldn't ring before because I've been busy, believe it or not. There's a turn up for the books! Busy! I've got a job – would you credit it? A small job, a tiddly job as they go, and it won't last long, but, by gosh, it's work! I'm getting my hands dirty again. So come and see me on site, soon as you can. Where? Ah – Langley Manor. What's Langley Manor? you ask. Langley Manor, my dear Stella, is the National Staff Training Centre for the Southwest Building Society. And what does the Southwest Building Society have to do with rescue archaeology? Ah, well – what has happened is that most inconveniently for the Southwest Building Society the excavation for the foundations of the squash court in the grounds, which is apparently essential to the well-being of the trainees at Langley Manor, has turned up some medieval tiles and what looks like the foundations of an early chapel. And since the Southwest Building Society cannot afford to do what it would prefer to do and quietly immolate this tiresome evidence, for fear of adverse publicity, it has agreed to halt its building programme – grudgingly and with much talk of the appalling costs incurred – while rescue archaeology moves in to find out just what it is we have here. Come – it's good.

Stella located Langley Manor on her large-scale atlas of south-western England – a significant black blob, complemented by similar blobs elsewhere, the Houses and Courts and Parks. There they were, the great houses of the county, each presiding over its neighbourhood, an extinguished social structure preserved thus on the page. For none of these Tudor, Georgian or Victorian piles was any longer the focus of local power and prestige. Many were still large-scale employers, but reborn as nursing homes, conference centres or country house hotels. Defrocked, they sat there in the landscape as architectural incongruities, out of scale and out of step. It was only on the map that they came back into perspective, each of them seen to be at the hub of its neighbourhood, lording it over the attendant villages and hamlets. A few were serving the heritage industry and raking in the shekels, tricked out with some zebras and buffalo or a miniature railway. All still in business, one way or another, but a far cry from their original purpose as social indicators.

Langley Manor was approached through parkland, the winding road allowing the visitor to appreciate stands of fine trees and grazing cattle before it straightened out into an avenue lined with chestnuts, displaying the distant façade of a Jacobean mansion. An array of signs indicated car-parks for Visitors, for Staff, Coffee Shop, Restaurant, Tennis Courts, Putting Green. The logo of the building society was prominent. Geraniums blazed in geometrical beds. The lawns were shaven carpets.

Stella parked her car and was directed by an attendant – also sporting the logo – to gravelled paths leading through gardens: 'You'll find them beyond the rose walk and the gazebo.' The flunkeys simply wear a different uniform, she thought. Commerce takes over where the aristocracy left off. This place – this entire landscape, indeed – was a subtle fusion of what was and what now is. And what now obtains is what matters – the rest is ballast, or backdrop, or the submerged seven-eighths of the iceberg. On the whole, this has been the case wherever Stella looked. In Malta or the Delta or Greece or indeed Orkney the crucial issue for most people was whether or not they had a firm grasp on the twentieth century, by way of access to petrol-driven vehicles and an improved diet, quite as much as the defence of customary practices and beliefs. There was she, pestering people about their lineage patterns and their neighbourhood structures when half the time what they themselves were exercised about was the fact that they had not yet achieved a transistor radio or a motorized scooter.

She found Judith squatting amid rubble, attended by a bunch of students, all of them stained pink with Somerset mud.

'Hello there! Six more tiles today and we think we've got the outline of the perimeter wall. We'll take our lunch break while you're here and I'll give you a run down.'

The students wandered off. Stella and Judith sat in the gazebo.

'Happy?' said Stella.

'Like a pig in clover. This only came my way because the young turks are all off at a Roman site that's been turned up under the new motorway spur. The kids are on loan from the University. It's a question now of fighting the building society for time. Men in dark suits keep coming to peer disconsolately, pretending to be interested.'

'When we first knew each other you were a young turk yourself, I suppose. On that Malta dig.'

'But it never felt like that at the time, did it? The first dig I was ever on, the director tried to sleep with me. A Cambridge professor, at that.'

'Did he succeed?'

'Certainly not. Though I considered it, in the interests of my career.' Judith laughed. 'Anyway, I was in love with one of the other academics and she wouldn't even look at me.'

'So what is this thing you're rescuing here?'

'It's a twelfth-century chapel. Associated undoubtedly with the priory that was on this site until it was knocked down for the building of the big house.'

'And what will happen to it?'

'Oh, it'll get buried under their wretched squash court. But I hope not before we've rescued any artefacts there may be and uncovered enough to make a plan of the structure. Anyway . . . it's been my salvation. I was at a very low ebb.'

'Your hands are certainly good and dirty now. You're eating Somerset earth with your sandwich. Which looks delicious.'

'Have one. Mary made them.'

'Mary well?'

'Mary's fine,' said Judith shortly. A pause. 'Actually, there's something I've been wondering about . . .' She broke off – a change of mind, it would seem – and began to talk about the excavation. The tiles must be survivors from the original floor. Judith's hope was that they might turn up fragments of worked stone to indicate the internal layout. She needed to get into a library to bone up – this wasn't her field at all.

'Sorry . . . blathering on like this. I get obsessed. So what's been happening with you?'

'I, too, have been applying myself,' said Stella. 'I have been thinking about gender and field-work.' She described her article. 'And how would that tally with your professional experience?'

'Oh, sex is a central concern in archaeology. All those hot nights under the stars. But of course the objects of study aren't around to complicate things. It's nicely straightforward and enlivens many a dig.'

'This is a serious piece I'm writing,' said Stella.

'Of course it is.' A propitiatory grin. 'And I am frivolous. Actually, some of your gripes apply. Machinery. Though I'm better than you at unreliable cars. Remember that heap we hired to drive around Italy?'

'Vividly.'

But it is not the image of the car that is lodged in Stella's head so much as that of Judith herself. Judith is wearing shorts and a skimpy black top. She is darkly tanned. They are somewhere in southern Italy, stuck once more at the side of an unfrequented, shadeless, dusty road with the temperature in the nineties. Judith is bent over the bonnet. When she looks up her face is streaked with oil where she has wiped away the sweat.

'Blast the internal combustion engine,' she says. 'If we were Romans, we'd be there by now. On foot. No damn spark plugs or batteries.'

Cropped dark hair. Wiry sunburnt limbs. Something androgynous about her, thinks Stella. Timeless, too. She could be anyone, any time, in this place. Were it not for the car. This hopeless Fiat or whatever it is.

' . . . looking for that Roman amphitheatre,' said Judith. 'Stuck by the road with the thing conked out again and then that guy with a truck turned up and towed us to the next village where his second cousin was the local mechanic. And you tried to talk to him in awful Italian about what was what in this village in darkest Calabria.'

'I did?' said Stella.

'You did indeed. I saw a field trip looming. My God, I thought, we've got to get out of here.'

This man is no longer there. Nor the conversation. Being towed over bumpy roads by a battered truck, yes, dimly. Loud and clear, on the other hand, is an old woman in black standing beside the car – the confounded Fiat or whatever – and holding forth in incomprehensible dialect. She makes gestures. There is a man in jeans and a grubby white vest who laughs and interprets. He is the mechanic. The old lady is his grand-mother. She is blessing the car.

'She may as well,' says Judith. 'A bit of extra insurance. If anyone has a line to the Almighty in these parts, I should think she has.'

' . . . the old lady who blessed the car,' said Stella.

'Really? Her I've forgotten entirely. Anyway, it got us to the Roman site. That's as clear as day.'

But not to Stella. Just a hazy impression of hard blue sky, the surprising curve of ruins against a hillside, Judith scrambling hither and thither.

It is moth-eaten, this fabric of the past. But Stella's moth holes do not coincide with Judith's moth holes, it would seem. Of course not. Unreliable witnesses, all of us. We select the evidence, or something does.

'Hey – how did we get on to this?' said Judith. 'We were talking about your article, I thought. Which I'd like to read. Anyway, I must get back to the job in hand. Here come the kids. Hang around for a bit if you've got nothing better to do.'

So Stella stayed for a while to watch this strange and reassuring process of meticulous recovery, while somewhere nearby a lawnmower purred over the lawns and the distant chock of croquet mallets backed by cries of distress indicated that the Southwest Building Society trainees were nicely into traditional country house pastimes during their leisure hours. Judith and her assistants brushed soil from fragments of ancient walling; within the Manor initiates contemplated banks of computer screens. Stella sat in the gazebo and considered this interesting juxtaposition of activities until her own failure to contribute to either began to induce guilt. When she said goodbye, Judith was too absorbed to make a more than perfunctory response.

Turning off the road and on to the lane she found herself confronted by a Hiscox tractor, roaring down upon her. She pulled into the passing place to let it by and caught a glimpse of Ted Hiscox in the cab, staring dourly ahead.

They'd had a real set-to, their parents. She had begun it, of course. Going on about money. Most of it the boys missed, because it wasn't a good thing to hang about when there was a row going on, but they heard bits through the open window. 'This place was bought with my money and just you remember that . . . if it wasn't for me, you'd be down at the Job Centre . . . it's me keeps this business going. Who does the accounts? Who got the loan from the bank?' Their father didn't put up much of a showing. Just 'Shut up! Shut up, will you! Belt up, for Christ's sake!' She always won in a fight – with anyone, at home or outside – just because she never let up. She could shout anyone down. Eventually the other person had had all they could stand and backed off. Like animals. You saw animals doing that. Dogs fighting – the one that goes on and on and the one that gives up.

Their father said, 'Shut up! Just bloody shut your mouth!' one last time and then packed it in. Went out. The door slam made the whole bungalow shake. Into the tractor and off. Probably didn't even know where he was going – just had to get away from the place for a bit.

Chapter Fourteen

'I anticipate a spot of bother with your gutters,' said Richard. He stood in front of the cottage, staring up. 'Distinct evidence of blockage. Not to worry – easily seen to. I can put you in touch with someone who does that kind of thing.'

Gutters? Stella gazed, interrupted in the middle of other concerns. There he was on the doorstep, frowning at her roof. But of course, this is what householders talk to one another about. It is just that I am not aware of the dialectic.

'Ah,' she said. 'Right.'

'The angle of the chimney is a bit curious, when one comes to look closely. Did you have a survey?'

Survey? Stella struggles again. She had been in the middle of some revisions to her article. Her mind was full of gender in field-work. She hesitated.

'When you bought the place. Several sheets of paper which would have cited apparent defects,' Richard explained kindly.

'Oh, yes . . . there was something like that.'

'A good idea perhaps to cast your eye over it again at some point. See if the chimney features.'

He had a tool-kit in hand, the lawnmower in mind. She had not invited him. He had called by – 'on the off-chance' – and now she did not know whether to be irritated or amused. His clothes proclaimed his intentions – the deliberately selected gear of a white-collar worker about to undertake a blue-collar task. Slightly grubby trousers, sweater out at one elbow.

'Come on, then. Tea or coffee?'

Half an hour later Richard briskly admitted defeat. The mower required a spare part, which he would order and bring at a later date. 'I'm sorry. I'd hoped to fix it here and now.'

'Don't worry. I live quite happily with a shaggy lawn.' She saw his expression and laughed. 'You forget that you're dealing with someone unused to a settled existence. I don't take easily to property ownership.'

He considered this. 'Maybe it's because you've spent more time than most of us with those who don't have much.'

'Possibly. Though in my experience the less people own, the more furiously defensive they are about what they do have.'

'Children always seemed to me to have an intense and innate sense of personal possession. As a parent, you spend much energy trying to temper this.'

He had accepted a second cup of coffee. She saw him look around the room. Is he going to offer to come and redecorate for me, she wondered. And if so, what would I say?

'Marriage, oddly enough, blunts one's sense of mine and thine. Things become ours, instead,' he observed.

'It also fuels the acquisitive instinct, or so I understand. The married are the great consumers. I bet you are loaded down with possessions. I've travelled relatively lightly.'

'I've managed to shed some now.'

Tactless of me, thought Stella. Of course he has. Out of the family home, into that dapper little farmhouse. She searched for something to say in compensation. Nadine floated there again, gleefully feathering nests. Her room at college had cushions, a tray with a tray cloth, cups and saucers instead of mugs.

'Something of a relief, I find.' He glanced around the room again. 'What you have, if I may say so, seems to be a nice combination of what is necessary and what has accrued, as it were. That khelim rug is Egypt, I suppose. Your Maltese dolphin door knocker. Things accrue, in marriage, but also two people seem to need so much more than twice as much as one person does.'

When I'm married, Nadine used to say, aged twenty . . . when I'm married I'm going to have one of those sets of Danish dining-room chairs from Heals, and a Race sofa, and curtains from Liberty.

'I don't think I would ever have made the grade as a paid-up consumer,' said Stella. 'It's just as well I've never married.'

'Marriage is deeply corrosive, in many ways. Not least because it makes you unfit to live alone. I had not reckoned with that.'

He was looking now directly at Stella, but she was barely aware of what he said. Nadine swarmed into her head. Nadine's views on love and marriage.

'I'm in love,' says Nadine.

Stella does a finger count. 'One, two, three . . . That's the fourth time this year.'

'No. Second time for real. David Harrap and Bill Bates were passing fancies. It's only been the real thing twice. This time I'm dying of it, no question.'

'That man at Balliol?'

'Of course,' says Nadine. 'I hung around the Broad most of yesterday and saw him twice. The last time he looked at me, definitely. He's reading French, which is a problem. I'm going to have to get an essay subject that means the books are in the Taylorian.'

'Tricky, when we're doing English II this term. You could do the French Revolution special subject next year.'

'Next *year*!' shrieks Nadine. 'I can't wait till next year. Even next week is bad enough. I'll find a way.'

She will, too. Nadine is single-minded where love is concerned.

'You should try it more,' she scolds Stella. 'It's heaven. So exciting. Every day is a cliff-hanger – will you manage to see him or won't you? And then if things come to a head, it's sheer bliss. I'm a bit worried about this one. I'm not sure that he's that interested in women.'

'Ah . . .' says Stella.

The young of the fifties were perfectly *au fait* with homosexuality, but less inclined to identify it amongst themselves. Girls like Nadine and Stella, whose antennae were acute, simply knew to write off a certain kind of man where romance was concerned.

'No, no – not that. He's a rowing man – in the college First Eight. He's always in the King's Arms, apparently – but how am I to get in there?'

Again, women undergraduates of the period did not go unaccompanied into pubs. With a man, fine. Without one, a solitary girl would have to be very confident of identifying male friends immediately or risk grave embarrassment. A group of mutually supportive girls would prompt raised eyebrows.

'It's not fair,' fumes Nadine. 'They can go wherever they like.'

'Well,' says Stella, 'you're just going to have to spend a lot of time on the towpath. You can borrow my duffel coat if you like.'

'You're making fun of me. You don't know what it's like. Why doesn't it happen to you?'

'I believe in grand passion,' says Stella. 'I'm waiting for that.'

There is some truth in this. Stella perceives, perhaps rather more sharply than Nadine, that this stage of life is in many ways a rehearsal. One is gearing up for what is to come, flexing the muscles. Above all, one is trying out for size various aspects of personality. Stella is not very clear yet who she is.

'Oh, that,' says Nadine. 'That all ends in tears.' For an instant there is a glint of a later Nadine. 'You've got to find someone to marry, definitely. But marriage isn't about grand passion.'

'Hang on . . .' says Stella, who sees that more than one seminal point is raised here. 'First of all, you've just said you're in love, and where you're concerned that has always ended in tears rather than marriage so far. And what *is* marriage about, in that case? I mean, if it's not passion. There you are stuck with someone else for ever.'

Divorce is entirely familiar to the children of the fifties, but marriage is still viewed with disconcerting sobriety. It is seen as a permanent arrangement. Well, they will find out.

Nadine ducks the issue. 'Oh, marriage is for later. The thing right now is simply – men. Here we are, surrounded by them. Spoiled for choice. The point is to make the most of it – we're never going to have it so good again.'

She's right about that, at least.

*

'You were bucking the trend,' Stella heard Richard say.

'Sorry?'

'Not marrying. It does you credit. The pressure was on, back then.'

'For men, too?' she enquired. One never really thought about their side of it, at the time.

'Certainly. It was a wise career move, on the whole. You were seen as more stable if married. You'd made an investment, had more at stake.'

'Is that what it felt like?'

'No,' said Richard, rather impatiently. 'Not at twenty-five or whatever. It felt like falling in with an expected procedure. And having someone to go to bed with on a permanent basis. Nadine was very attractive.'

We're getting a bit near the knuckle, thought Stella. Positively confessional. 'Of course she was. I've been thinking about her a lot lately.'

He shied away. 'I'll be off now, since I can be of no further use right now over the mower. The spare part shouldn't take too long. I'll bring the phone number for the chap who does the gutters.'

'Thanks,' said Stella. 'You'll make a householder of me yet.'

After he had gone she found herself thinking not of lawn-mowers or gutters but of Nadine again. Had Nadine continued to fall in love four times – sorry, twice – a year after her marriage to Richard? Patently not. Nadine had reinvented herself, as wife, mother and responsible citizen. Her letters had been full of Consumer Groups, protests against road schemes and campaigns for nursery schools. The skirmishes of love had been a necessary rite of passage, that was all.

And I conjure up Nadine, thought Stella, because to do so

174

is also to conjure up myself. There seems to be this compulsion to take stock, to see from whence and from what one has come. To look at the old photos.

'So how are you, then?' said Molly in the shop. 'Good. I've kept you a *Herald*. You forgot to pick it up last week. Not a thing I like to be without, myself. The national papers you can keep, but you don't know what's going on without the *Herald*. The cottage by the church is for sale, I see. People don't stay put nowadays, do they? It's here today and gone tomorrow. Didn't used to be like that, round here. Still isn't, for some, if you see what I mean – ' a momentary pause within which Stella is subtly defined and perhaps delicately distanced – 'but that being said, there's those that muck in and pull their weight and those that don't. You used to know how a person stood, without having to take soundings, know what I mean? You knew if they were farming or trade, church or chapel, you knew who their father was and which way they'd jump if it came to the push. Nowadays, people can walk into the shop and it's anyone's guess, frankly . . . Not that that doesn't have its own interest, mind. Still, it's complicated. Even the *Herald* doesn't help there.' She laughed.

Naturally, thought Stella, getting into the car. All societies are complex, most are opaque – a fact which has kept the likes of me in business for quite a while now. But I am no longer in business, I am a part of the landscape like everyone else. And some of us are more tenuously placed within that landscape than others. Some are entrenched; others merely perch.

All her life, wherever she was, she had thought of herself as a bird of passage. She had rented rooms or flats, expecting to move on. Where she worked, most of her colleagues were sunk deep in the culture of mortgages and house prices; she had felt relief to be excused all that. And in the field she had been in the ultimate state of transience – the invisible observer, the visitor from outer space. The people in whom she was interested were there, in that place – she herself was both there and crucially apart. If she lived permanently anywhere, it was in a landscape of the mind.

In the Delta village no one knew where England was, except that it was distant. For most Maltese the general impression of Australia, to which many of their friends and relations had emigrated, was that it could not be that far away, since they knew that it took only twenty-four hours or so to get there. Orcadians refer to Scotland as the south. The siting of else-where depends on the viewpoint, but in the last resort it is simply elsewhere, with all that that implies. We are here but they are there, where things are done differently.

She drove home. The red car tore past her on the lane, belching exhaust fumes. Karen Hiscox raised a hand in per-functory greeting.

The boys considered one another. Furtively, but each knowing that the other was doing it. That complementary face – the same thick dark brows, blunt nose, jut of the chin.

I hate her, they told each other.

'Maybe they gave me the wrong ones at the hospital.' That's what she'd said. 'It happens. You don't look like me, do you? Neither of you.'

It did not occur to them that this was disproved by their resemblance to one another. They were slow thinkers. Later, at some point, they stumbled to this realization, but by then the incident was just part of a general cargo of resentment.

*

'It's going well,' said Judith. 'Far too well, so far as the Southwest Building Society is concerned. Two more trenches and I think we shall have most of the perimeter wall. The Southwest Building Society comes along in its pin-stripe suits and gazes in dismay. It sees its squash court receding by the day. The local paper did three columns and a nice picture of my students digging away in shorts and T-shirts. That's bought me another week or two at least. No way the pin-stripes can move us on while that's fresh in the local mind. I'm considering school visits and an Open Day. Come and visit again. Bring your boyfriend. Interested crowds are what I need. Sorry, did you say something? Joke, joke . . . You said yourself he keeps offering services. Seriously, though, noise it abroad. ELECTRIFYING DISCOVERY OF TWELFTH-CENTURY CHAPEL UNDER SQUASH COURT FOUNDATIONS. It's the only way we'll buy more time. What? No, medieval chapels are not two-a-penny, even in these parts. Even the pin-stripes know better than to suggest that. Oh . . . joke, I see. All right – *touché*. But what would really serve the purpose is a burial. No, you idiot – an *ancient* burial. Medieval graveyard, that's what I want. Bring in the demographic boys and I'd be in business for months. No, I shouldn't think there's much chance. Best we can do is scrape on and hope for . . . You've just heard what? Shots? Well, people do shoot things in the country, don't they? It's the main point of the place, as I understand it. So anyway, get over if you can, otherwise I'll give you a ring again. Have to go now. Mary wants me to give her a hand with something . . .'

The boys went a little way up the grass track to the hills. They had a go at some pigeons and then a crow, but didn't get anything. And they didn't dare stay long – their parents were both out, but their mother could be back any time. Michael cleaned the gun and hung it up again in her study. They were both shaking, in case she came. But it was worth it. It gave them a buzz, all evening, knowing what she didn't know. She thought she knew everything about them, did she? Well, there were things she didn't know.

'I've picked up the throttle cable,' said Richard. 'I could stop by and fit it one day next week, if that suits you. So ... how are things with you? Excellent. Oh, not too bad ... My self-imposed schedule. The days are filled, one way and another. A determined assault on old papers, at the moment. A task I've been postponing. Including things of Nadine's I felt unable to deal with when ... at the time. Apropos of which, there is the occasional communication from yourself. I'll bring them along, shall I? Ah ... right, then, I won't. You, too, are de-accessioning – I believe that's the archivists' term. I will consign to black sacks. Mostly postcards from exotic locations, anyway. One from Orkney with picture of seal and pups and cryptic message on the reverse – "Time for a five-year check? Long days to be seized up here." No doubt you could deconstruct. I read it – hope you share my view that postcards are in the public domain.'

'The thing about life is to have a strategy,' says Nadine. 'Ultimate aim, fall-back position. The aim right now is Magdalen Commem with John Hobhouse, but if he doesn't ask me, then I'll have to settle for David Phelps, who will if I throw out a hint. And here are you in the fifth week of term with no strategy at all. Do you want David if I don't need him? I could probably fix it.'

'No thanks,' says Stella. 'At the worst I'll pass up Magdalen Commem. And in any case I entirely disagree. The thing about life is to act expediently and creatively. Seize the day. See what comes up and act accordingly.'

'Fatal. Drift theory. That way you get stuck doing things you never meant to do and you end up married by accident to the wrong person or not married at all when you're *thirty*.'

'Or,' says Stella, 'you proceed from one glittering opportunity to the next and are mercifully still available for grand passion when the moment strikes.'

'We'll see,' says Nadine. 'We'll see. Wanna bet?'

'Bet on what? How are we to decide who is coming off best?'

'Five-year checks,' proposes Nadine. 'Absolute honesty on both sides. I chalk up strategic success and you prove opportunistic gains.'

Peter said to their father, 'Where was I born? And Michael?'

'What d'you mean? In a hospital, of course.'

'But where? What town?'

'Dunno. Can't remember. Wherever we was then.'

'Did you have that garage when we were born?'

'Maybe. Shut up asking stupid questions and do something useful. You can start changing that wheel.'

Like you'd slammed up against a brick wall. He'd always been like that, their father, but even more now. Not a word, most of the time. Eat, go out to the sheds, go off on a job, come back, eat.

Her, you knew about, because she told you, when she felt

like it. She'd been on that ranch in America and she'd been at a college and she'd done racing driving and run businesses with a turnover of thousands. At least, that's what she said. Their father, you didn't know anything.

'And us,' said Peter. 'We dunno where we were fucking born. Not even that.'

'Yeah.'

They couldn't have said why it mattered. Simply, they lacked something. There was nothing they could cite. Other people came from round here, or they didn't. And if they didn't, they knew where they'd been. The boys saw that they were without a history, though they were unable to identify the perception.

Nadine searches for Stella in the Radcliffe Camera. She sweeps past the desks wearing her red crossover jersey and her flared grey flannel skirt, causing heads to lift, distracting keen young minds from the significance of the Exchequer under Edward I, from the role of Ship Money, from the rise of Chartism. She beams at friends and acquaintances. She locates Stella. '*There* you are. Come and have coffee. I've got things to tell.'

Nadine has been to the Oxford University Appointments Board. 'The woman went berserk,' says Nadine. 'I was honest and straightforward. I said, I just want a nice interesting job for a couple of years because I intend to get married shortly. And she blew up. I'm planning on having children in good time, I said. And she said, you haven't been expensively educated here for three years in order to have children.'

'No, she didn't,' says Stella, who knows Nadine.

'Well, that's what she was thinking. "What sort of job did you have in mind?" she asked. Clipped voice. Freezing stare.

And I suggested something where you meet lots of people and there's opportunity for travel.'

'Air hostess,' says Stella. 'Package-tour guide.'

'Certainly not. Marry a diplomat, possibly. So then she wanted what are apparently called my credentials and I don't seem to have any. Apart from the degree that we sincerely hope I will indeed get. You're supposed to have run for President of the JCR or written for *Isis* or been a stage manager for OUDS. She wanted to know what I was interested in.'

'So you said – men.'

Nadine giggles. 'She gave me more of the cold stare and said, I advise you to do a course in shorthand and typing. So *I* gave *her* a look and said, surely I haven't spent three years being expensively educated here in order to become a secretary?'

'Spot on!' says Stella, admiring. Just occasionally, Nadine can score a bull's-eye.

Chapter Fifteen

Stella had not at first realized that there was a fifth person living at the Hiscox bungalow. But then she once or twice caught sight of a white head in the back seat of the red car. Someone's old mother, presumably. Occasionally the two boys would also be in the car, but generally speaking it was rare to see members of the family except in isolation – an expressionless profile hurtling past in car or tractor or pick-up van, the boys hunched over the handlebars of their bicycles. Stella was faintly bothered by the thought of this concealed old woman, stashed away there like an obsolete piece of furniture except for these infrequent airings. She thought of old people in the Delta village or in Malta, intently monitoring local life from a chair outside the front door. Far more rewarding than the television set in a nursing home. Or whatever fetid family life was experienced by this poor old soul.

A life that must be at its most intense now in late July with the school holidays in full swing. The Hiscox boys were more in evidence than usual, mooching up and down the lane on foot or on the bikes, tinkering with a tractor on the track to the bungalow. Indeed, the whole landscape seemed to run with young, like fields in the lambing season – every recreation ground swarming, gangs of children erupting round corners, silting up the village newsagent in pursuit of snacks.

There was a group of adolescents eddying around the phone box on the green as she headed for the car after visiting the shop. Half a dozen boys and a clutch of girls, grouping and regrouping, several of the boys equipped with sleek cycles on which they made occasional flamboyant circuits, like cock birds displaying. The girls tossed their hair, preened self-conscious bodies, draped themselves against a fence. The air crackled with sexuality. Stella observed, amused. So it goes, she thought, the world over.

And now their collective attention was diverted. They were watching two boys who had emerged from the newsagent's, mounted bikes and started to ride away. Ah, the Hiscox lads. Who were not, it would seem, part of the gang, for they pointedly ignored the group on the green, a ploy which at once provoked a response. The girls clustered together, giggling and staring. Jeering derisive shouts from the boys. A cat-call, a whoop. The general tenor of rejection was clear enough. The Hiscox boys were approaching her now, pedalling fast, their expressions tense and sullen. She smiled, in a sudden access of sympathy. 'Hi, there!' she called out. No reply. Black scowls and they were gone, rattling away down the road. On the green there were gusts of laughter; the sexual parade had resumed.

The village green was a triangle. Stella had read somewhere that its shape echoed the structure of the original medieval settlement, with an enclosed central area in which animals could be safely penned. Today, one end was laid out as a children's playground with swings and slides, while the tele-phone kiosk commandeered by the adolescents occupied the apex of the triangle. Facing on to it were the pub, the garage, the Minimart, the chemist, a diminutive branch of Barclay's

Bank, a sprig of the West Country's main estate agents and a solicitor's office. The green was always the scene of various concurrent actions, most of them mutually exclusive. The adolescents ignored the group of mothers with small children, who were in turn impervious to Stella, passing them on her way back to the car. She herself, she realized, should find an affinity with the several other visible grey heads. The retired, the settlers, the colonizers.

But I do not, she thought. Cannot. Nothing in common except physical condition. Flung into proximity by circumstance, like children. But then I have never had much talent for belonging.

Most people require a support base – family, community. Everyone does, perhaps. The extension of oneself that allows 'me' to dissolve into 'us', that supplies common cause and provides opportunity for altruism and reciprocal favours and also for prejudice, insularity, racialism, xenophobia and a great deal else. Most people are either born into this situation or achieve it, by hook or by crook.

Except for me, thought Stella. Unwed, peripatetic. By choice and by chance. Spending my time taking stock of how others deal with proximity, while avoiding it myself. So am I a freak? Dangerously deprived? I passed up the offer of both, once.

'Marry me,' says Alan Scarth, 'and you'll see this every year of your life.'

The sea cliff to which the island rises has sprung alive. It has bloomed with birds. They are nesting – the kittiwakes and the guillemots and the razorbills and the fulmars. They pack each ledge, each slope, each pinnacle. The entire sheer surface of the rock is studded with ranks of white, with clusters of black. More birds float alongside, sliding on the wind, swerving and twisting, rising and falling. The sea and the air are spawning birds, they lift from the waves, they surge from the spray.

'You promised you wouldn't say that again,' says Stella. 'You're a man of your word, I thought. Known for it, I'm told.'

'I had my fingers crossed,' says Alan Scarth.

He is also a man of absolute propriety. He has never touched her. Even here, side by side on the turf amid the thrift and the sea-campion, he keeps a clear space between them. Once he laid a hand on her back to steady her over a stile. She seemed to feel its burning imprint for hours.

'Teach me which are what,' says Stella. 'Is that big dark one a skua?'

'Marry me and I'll teach you.'

'No,' says Stella. 'I've told you why. It would be the ruin of us both. Where are the puffins?'

'You're an obstinate woman and opinionated with it,' says Alan. 'There are some puffins left of the big stack in the centre. Track past those kittiwakes, then go down to the next level.'

'I've got them,' says Stella.

She is intensely conscious of his solid presence, a foot away. As stable as the rock, as assured as his tenure of this place. He occupies it like the birds – by right, by nature. Am I making a terrible mistake? she wonders. Could I be like that, too?

The summer days flow one into another through the brief hours of dusk that pass for night. Just as the great skies melt into the sea and the land on cloudy days, a symphony of grey, no distinction between the elements. Time is on hold, it seems, its passage marked only by hay-making, by harvest. The people of the island work and Stella works alongside, with her note-book and her queries, her lists and her charts. The summer unfurls for her not in weeks or months but by the way in which she is subsumed into the lives of these people, by their kindly acceptance of what she does, by their interest. They are mildly amused to be the objects of study. They, too, ask questions, which give pause for thought.

'And how will this make the world a better place?' asks Alan Scarth. Tongue in cheek, perhaps. Back in the early days, back when he was just another face to be learned and filed away in the head, another name for the card index.

She has explained to him that her project is an element of a wider study that aims to gather data on the absorption of immigrant arrivals into isolated and enclosed communities. Communities such as townships in remote parts of Canada and the United States. Societies such as those of the Hebrides or of this Orkney island to which, over time, outsiders have come. To this end she must plot the network of relationships, she must seek to understand the structure of the society – its attitudes, its assumptions, its codes.

It won't do anything to save the world, Stella replies. Or only in that it might be a tiny contribution to the process of understanding why human beings carry on as they do.

'Well, never mind all that for now,' says Alan Scarth. 'It's a beautiful evening. Come for a walk and I'll show you the seals.'

Seals sing. She had not known that. They make this plaintive eerie musical sound – woo-woo-woo – which floats unearthly from the shore. Later, her head is full of this, and the bird cries and the waves creaming on to a crescent of silver sand. She thinks also of Alan Scarth's question. But she thinks of it in drowsy comfort, not as a challenge but as an endorsement of her presence here. She feels as though she were a roosting bird, come homing in to this bare, stark, glorious place of wind and water. She has a little stone house in which she burns peat of an evening and lights the oil-lamp. She has oyster-catchers and curlews outside her windows and her nearest neighbour is half a mile away, a farmer by name of Alan Scarth.

A great bear of a man with a flaming mane of hair. Even his eyebrows are ginger-gold, and the hairs on his arms.

Hair, indeed, unites them on their first meeting. He interrupts Stella's queries about island practices to point at her head – a stubby, calloused, peremptory forefinger. 'You've an Orkney look about you. Were your parents from the north?'

'I'm afraid not,' says Stella. Noting as she speaks that she is in some obscure way apologizing for this. And she has only been here a week. Such is the power of the place.

He seems to fill the room, that first time he ducks under the low lintel to ask if she is getting along all right. He sits there at the table with the old webbed yellow oilcloth, accepts a mug of tea and extracts from her an account of herself while she is barely aware of giving it. He is there – huge, intent, his blue eyes fixed upon her – and then he is gone. 'I'll be seeing more of you,' he says from the door.

He is a farmer. But he is also a polymath, she is to discover, a Jack-of-all-trades. He is an archetype, the stuff from which farmers are made, a man free in time and space. He can turn his hand and his strength to anything. He is Hercules, he is a Viking. He can plough a field, row a boat, cut peat, mend a tractor. He can tell what the weather will do, and when and where the sea is safe. He knows about beef and sheep and crops, about plants and birds, about the ancestry of this green slab of land in a shining sea. Give him a piece of machinery and he will perceive at once how it works and see how to fix it if it doesn't. He is a man who comes from other times, Stella realizes, from worlds where you had to be able to do anything or you would not survive. He is the frontiersman, the pioneer. If required, he could have discovered the North-West Passage, trekked to California, colonized Australia.

Stella seizes the day. The summer days in Orkney, which are twenty-four hours long, where sunset blends with dawn. She learns to love the weather. The wind and the mist. The sun that paints the sea with bands of turquoise. The rolling clouds that sweep great veils of rain across the island. She decides that heat and dust are not necessary adjuncts to study. One could become addicted to the social anthropology of a cold climate.

'In the winter,' says Alan Scarth, 'you get the big sea fogs. There's darkness at noon, in winter, some days. Then we light the lamps and read a book. You'll like that, Stella.'

There are many books in Alan's farmhouse. Rows of big solid sober books he had from his father. Dog-eared paperbacks that cascade from tables, that line the staircase. There is a kitchen with a stone-flagged floor on which the farm dogs slump, a dresser with ranks of flowered plates that belonged to his grandmother.

'Alan, I'll not be here in the winter,' says Stella.

'I can't hear you,' says he. 'Terrible racket this old stove makes. Maybe I'll get a new one. Now a Rayburn's the thing, they say, isn't it?'

*

They say, too, that Alan Scarth could have had his pick of the girls. Stella learns this because those who are generous in response to her questionnaires, are sometimes so enthusiastic that the information given spills far beyond the parameters of the questions asked. Thus she hears much that is in theory irrelevant to her researches. She hears how young Annie Flett sneaked on to the boat and got herself to Kirkwall, aged ten. She hears how there's been quite a few set their cap at Alan Scarth, but here he is, forty-five and still on his own.

'Marry me,' says Alan. This is the third time.

'No,' says Stella.

He stares at her, as though willpower might do the trick. As well it might – she looks away.

'It wouldn't work,' says Stella. 'Can't you see? I don't belong here.'

'You like it here. You like me. Don't you?'

'Yes,' says Stella. 'Yes and yes. But that's not enough.'

'You'll go south,' says Alan. 'And that'll be that.'

'I'll come back,' says Stella. 'We'll always be friends.'

Alan laughs. But he is not amused. 'I don't want us to be friends. I want us to be married.'

Alan Scarth has been south. He has been to university at Aberdeen, which was well enough, he says, the books he enjoyed and the beer wasn't bad, but he didn't stay there a minute longer than he had to. When Stella hears this, she nods in agreement. Of course, it could not be otherwise. She tries to imagine Alan in Aberdeen, in the grey streets. Like a great young bull he must have been, pent up.

And then his father had died, not long after, so he had to

take over the farm. And his mother moved to Kirkwall, to be near her sister, who had married a Kirkwall man, way back. So there he was in the big farmhouse, on his own, with the girls eyeing him, and it, and the dresser with the flowered plates (this he does not state but it can be inferred).

Nothing like this has ever arisen before. It is a complication passed over in the textbooks, in the classic accounts of field-work. Nowhere does it say that emotional involvement with the subjects of study is inadvisable. Unprofessional. Indeed, nowhere does it say that you cannot marry them, should the question come up.

Furthermore, Stella cannot help but note from her gathering piles of notes, of cards, of names and dates, that incomers are indeed digested into this place. The extent and manner of this digestion is, after all, central to her project. People arrive. Not all of them leave again. And those who stay become a part of the texture of the place, in one way or another.

So?

She recognizes that she has landed at one of those alarming junctions in life, where decision is treacherous, where alternative existences stream into an unimaginable future. So she tries to avoid the issue by living from day to day, with relish, with fervour. She brims with energy, she could walk over the horizon, she feels.

On many of these days she is with Alan Scarth, as the summer pitches ahead, open-ended, perilous.

'Listen,' says Stella. 'If I married you, we'd be eyeball to eye-ball, day in, day out. With both of us the people we are. Think of it.'

There is a gleam of satisfaction in his eye. A foxy look. 'Ah,' he says. 'That's what I want to hear. If . . .'

'Purely hypothetical,' says Stella. 'I'm merely trying to make you see why it's got to be out of the question.'

'You're failing entirely,' says he. 'And you with all that academic training. Now I'm just a simple man, but I know a good proposition when I see one.'

Simple, indeed, thinks Stella. Simple my foot. Clever, resourceful, ingenious. Straightforward. Complex. At this precise moment – disarming, persuasive.

'Look,' she says. 'I work. What would I do here?'

He has thought of that. He is one step ahead. You could come and go, he tells her. Go south when you need to. Do your field trips. Come back up here for your writing, your studying. I'd settle for that.

She pounces. Maybe you would, she says to him, but would everyone else? It's not the way things are done up here and you know that. I'd be the weak link and you'd suffer for it.

'Then I'll suffer gladly,' says he. 'If need be. But I think you're wrong. You'd fit here well enough.'

'Look at us now,' says Stella. 'We're quarrelling.'

'All married people quarrel,' says he.

'Why me?' she asks him. 'When there's half the girls in Orkney after you. Or so I'm told.'

'Because you're not like any woman I ever met. Because you've got red hair, so you belong here anyway.'

Occasionally Stella reminds herself that the rest of the world exists by writing a letter, or a postcard. She writes a letter to her friend Judith, who is digging up the past somewhere in

Turkey. She sends a postcard to her friend Nadine. There is a choice of three cards in the island shop: sunset over Scapa Flow, puffins on a crag, or female seal with pup. She selects the seals and writes a message on the back which may or may not stir in Nadine a memory of a conversation they once had, way back, time out of mind ago, when they were quite other people, when all the roads lay open, when choice was so prodigal that it held no terrors.

Sometimes when she is with Alan Scarth the air is taut with what is not said. Sex is unspoken, but it is ripe between them. It is a sizzling force-field to be skirted, it is the silent sub-text. Marry me, he says, and he means it. Come to bed with me, he does not say, because this is more important than immediate gratification and he has the long view in mind. But she can feel him reined in, tense with control. And sometimes it is as much as she can do not to reach out, to put a hand on his burning flesh, to say – yes, me too, you are not alone in this.

Does she love him? All she knows is that some cautionary instinct tells her it would never do, it would come undone, it would scupper them both. In the midst of all this heightened time there is a sane and fatal voice which tells her, no. You wouldn't last, not the way you are. The two of you would never last, with him the way he is, with this place the way it is.

'So you'll not marry me,' says Alan Scarth.

She is silent. Time has run out. The summer has fetched up against autumn. She has her bags packed, her notebooks, her card indexes. She would pack what she is feeling, too, if she could, this hard cold lump in the belly.

'You'll regret it,' says he.

'Possibly. Probably, even. But we'd both regret it even more if I did. Believe me.' She cannot look at him so she looks instead at the sea cliff, from which the birds are now gone, the mob, the multitude, that teeming life. Just a few left, floating against the rock face, skimming the waves.

'I'm sorry,' she says. The words break in the middle – she hears her voice as though it were someone else's.

He reaches out to her. The first time. He takes her hand in his. 'There it is, then,' he says. 'There it is, then, Stella.'

When Stella thought now of those months, they had still that sense of a continuous present. And Alan Scarth was frozen in her head as he was then – that fiery, potent giant of a man in the prime of his life. Herself she could not see, because that Stella was eclipsed entirely by subsequent Stellas and above all by the Stella of today, who confronted her from the mirror, features distorted by age, body softened and sagging. Very occasionally, she would be shocked to think that he also, if he was out there still, must now be thus.

She had never been back to the island. For a year or two after that summer they had exchanged occasional letters, and then the exchange had shrunk to anodyne postcards written by Stella, to which he ceased to reply. And it was better so, she would think. By now one of those opportunist local lasses must have got her way, and good luck to her. More fool me, perhaps.

Except that she had known herself to be driven by some submerged wisdom. She could mourn that lost experience, the vibrancy of that summer, the person that she had been, but she could not anguish over a mistake. The time shone out now as one of heightened living, not as lost opportunity.

There it is, she thought. As he said. There it is. I had my chance to belong – to belong to someone, to belong somewhere. And passed it up. For good reason. Knowing myself. Knowing the expectations of a place like that, which I could not have met.

She drove away from Kingston Florey with her head full of that other community, far more inflexible, far more impregnable. She had been intending to go back to the cottage, where the dog was shut in and would be desperate for an outing. But as she reached the entrance to the track, she changed her mind. It was hot, a walk up the mineral line seemed suddenly unappealing – overgrown at this time of year and the bracken full of flies. The dog could wait until later in the day. She would visit Judith at her dig.

The Hiscox boys on their bikes were just turning into the track as she passed. She smiled again and lifted her hand from the wheel in greeting. They swung their heads sideways and glared at her. She remembered the mocking adolescents. Poor little tykes.

Chapter Sixteen

There'd been a bunch of them on the green – two people from school and others they didn't know. And girls. Stupid cows. Michael and Peter tried to get past quickly but the others saw them. They'd known what would come and it did. Shouting things about their fucking bikes. And about them, too. And the girls hearing and laughing. Silly fucking cows. And then they'd seen the woman from the cottage and she was grinning away too and saying something.

Afterwards they told each other that they should have ridden into her. Given her something to think about.

They didn't give a shit about girls anyway. Some of the boys at school went on about it all the time. Who they'd done it with, how often they'd done it. So what? What was the big deal?

Stupid bitches.

They rode back and then just before they turned off the road into the lane, there she was again, the woman from the cottage, driving past. Looking towards them and pointing. Grinning. Pointing at their bikes.

She didn't turn in to go home but went off down the main road and when she was out of sight, Peter looked over his shoulder at Michael and said, 'You seen that? You seen what she did?'

'Yeah. She'll be sorry. We'll see to it she's sorry.'

They went to the cottage without really knowing what they were going to do, except that she wasn't there, so there'd be something they could do. She'd driven off, so it was safe enough. They walked around to the back, thinking that they'd maybe break a window. The stupid dog was scrabbling away at the glass doors into the garden, barking. Peter rattled at the handle to get it worked up and to their surprise the door opened. It wasn't locked. The dog flew out, barking and jumping up. Michael kicked it, as hard as he could, catching it a good thump in the belly and it belted off, squealing. They watched it run into the lane. And then Peter shut the door again and they made off. They knew suddenly what they were going to do. They didn't even have to talk about it.

'I'm really glad you've come,' said Judith. 'I was feeling some-what pissed off. I can see the end of this dig looming, for one thing. It seems impossible to screw another penny from anywhere and the building society is starting to breathe very heavily indeed. The pin-stripes are running out of patience and polite interest. Trouble is, I can't guarantee to come up with anything persuasively crucial in the immediate future. Burial ground? No such luck, I'm afraid. We've got the basic plan now, and some tiles and other bits and pieces, and they're going to close in on me and insist on their wretched squash court going ahead. I'd need weeks and months to be able to prove that there's more that should be excavated, which there probably is. So I can see the whole thing fizzling out, which is a shame. Other thing? Oh, well . . . life in general, I suppose, put it that way. I'm getting to the point where . . . Here, I'm not going to pile any of that on you . . . So how are things?

Good, good. You're looking very buoyant, if I may say so. Positively glowing. All in the mind, you say? Well, bully for you. It certainly suits you, whatever you've been mulling over. Hang on, I'll tell the kids they can take a break and we'll go to the pin-stripes' canteen and get a bite to eat.'

Michael shot the dog. They found it again quite quickly – stupid thing was wandering around by the track up to the hill and when it saw them, it came rushing up, tail wagging and all. Michael was the one holding the gun, so it was he got to shoot it. The first shot didn't kill it and it was thrashing around screaming, so Peter took the gun and gave it two more. They didn't have to worry about anyone hearing because their mother had gone to Taunton and their father was out on a job up on the Brendons.

Then they didn't know what to do. They felt good and they'd be one up on that silly old cow for ever now, but they could see this might mean trouble, one way or another. They couldn't leave the dog where it was, so they carried it a little way up the mineral line and stuffed it into the overgrown ditch. The woman would think it had just got out and run away. Got done for by a car or something.

But they'd know what really happened. Like they knew about other things.

'Don't get me wrong,' said Stella. 'I'm not talking about nostalgia, sentiment – that stuff. What I mean is . . . fishing out good times and . . . having a sort of re-run. It can give you such a lift . . . the peculiar way it's all still *there*. Not you? Oh, come on, it's just because you're feeling down. Think of Malta, that year. No, I wasn't, as it happens. Another time and place. Well, yes, someone else, if you like. No, the list of my past loves is not inexhaustible, what nonsense. Definitely finite. And in this case . . . But the point is this business of emotion recollected in tranquillity. Contradiction in terms? I disagree. Though, all right, maybe it's not tranquillity, exactly . . . Clarity, more. You see the thing clearly, which you don't at the time, when it's all helter-skelter feelings. I don't know why I'm going on like this. Well, you started me off . . . Anyway, I must go – I left the dog shut in and he'll be frantic. No, he's not a mistake, I like him, and anyway he gives me street credibility. I have a house, I have a significant domestic relationship, I'm a paid-up citizen for the first time in my life. And listen, I'm sorry about this dig folding up. It's really too bad. And whatever else it is you're . . . anyway, look, keep in touch, right?'

'Dogs do not open doors,' said Stella. 'Someone has been here.'

The policeman had patrolled both house and garden. She agreed with him that there was no indication of any break-in.

'And you're quite certain that the dog was shut in before you went out?' he said.

Stella hesitated – a small but perhaps betraying hesitation, which occurred not so much because she was in any doubt but because, if asked a question, she was in the habit of giving it due consideration. She saw at once in the policeman's face that he felt this whole matter to be a touch unsound. He closed his notebook, switched on his mobile phone and listened to a few seconds of unintelligible crackling. He was already moving on to the next local difficulty.

'It's conceivable that I forgot to bolt the French windows. But they certainly weren't left open.'

'I do advise you to lock up securely in future. Window locks would be a good thing, and a mortice on the front door. We'll be in touch if anything's heard of the dog. You could put an ad in the paper, someone may have spotted him . . .'

She saw him out, watched the police car turn towards the main road. Then she went and scoured the area again. Up the mineral line, right to the top. Nothing. The road, she thought. Undoubtedly. Picked off in the traffic. Poor little beggar. Oh, shit . . . She had already toured the lane, asking if anyone had seen the dog, and drawn a blank with each enquiry. There was no one around at the Hiscox place.

She would not have believed that you could feel so stricken. About an animal, for heaven's sake. The silence in the cottage, that evening. The void where there should have been that small, insistent presence. At one point she found her eyes welling with tears and was astonished. It came to her that there was an entire dimension of human emotion of which she had been ignorant. People were going through this on all sides and one had never realized. Cats, dogs, budgerigars, hamsters, heaven knows what. All leaving a bleak space in someone's life, triggering this disproportionate, lunatic response in otherwise balanced and reasonable adult women. And men, one must suppose.

She searched the fields again, walked again up the mineral line. She drove back and forth along the main road, looking fearfully for some dark bundle on the verge.

'But it'll just come back, won't it?' said Judith. 'Isn't that what dogs do? One's always reading about it in the tabloid press. People move house and the family pooch miraculously navigates a hundred miles down the M1 to the old place. That's cats? Well, I don't know about either, I must admit, and I'm sorry you're so cut up about it, but I mean, you'd only had it a few months . . . Sorry, sorry – no, I can see I don't understand, so I'd better shut up. I'm sure it'll reappear. Well, two days isn't *that* long . . .'

'You've advertised in the local paper?' said Richard. 'And a notice in the shop . . . right. Was it pedigree? I mean, would anyone want to steal it? Definitely not . . . well, that's all to the good, I imagine. Look, it may well turn up yet. Six days . . . Oh, I see. Look, I was calling in fact to say, should I come over to fix the mower? Well, no, I can see that under the circumstances your thoughts have not centred on grass-cutting, but life has to go on, I suppose. Oh dear, I didn't mean to sound brisk . . . No, we never had a dog. Any day this week I could do . . . Friday afternoon. Maybe you'll have had good news by then, who knows . . .'

The boys were in their room when the policeman came to the bungalow. It was quite early in the morning. She was getting breakfast – their father was in the kitchen too. They saw the police car from the window, saw the man get out, come up the path. Heard the knock. He'd come about the fires. Must have. He was in the kitchen now – they could hear voices. They went into the passage, quietly, and stood stock still behind the door, listening, their guts creeping. And then they heard her say, 'What dog? I don't know what you're talking about.' The boys understood now and their stomachs went back to normal. It was about the stupid dog – the woman's dog – and that didn't matter, at least not so much. They'd just say they didn't know anything about it, like she was.

The policeman said the dog had been reported missing and now someone walking up the mineral line had found its body. Another dog found it, sniffing around. Dog was shot, said the policeman. Dog belonging to the lady at Vine Cottage. Making enquiries. List at the station showed gun licence in the name of T. G. Hiscox.

She let fly. That really got up her nose. A policeman walking in like that. We don't know anything about any dog. What's it got to do with us if the dog got shot up on the mineral line? Plenty of people shooting around here, aren't there?

On and on. And the policeman backing off now, he wanted out. And then their father came into it. We don't know anything about anyone's sodding dog. Anything gets shot around our place it's the bloody pigeons, that's all. That's what the gun's for, isn't it? What's the fact that I've got a gun have to do with this dog getting shot?

The policeman seemed to feel the same, apparently, because he asked to check the gun licence and then went off.

The boys came into the kitchen. They were both thinking that they'd keep quiet, that would be the best thing. Just keep their heads down and there'd be no aggro.

Their father sat down and went back to his breakfast. That was that, far as he was concerned. But she was looking at them. Looking in a way they didn't like.

'You know anything about that dog?'

They stood there, mouths slammed shut. Michael shrugged. Say nothing and they'd be OK. It would be something else they knew about and no one else.

She went out of the room. Into the office. Came back, at once, and they saw in her face that she knew. How could she?

Neither of them spoke. They thought it, and she saw them thinking.

'Because you put it back the wrong way round, you stupid little gits. I can see someone's had it out.'

Now their father had banged down his knife and fork. They hit the wall, both of them. Who said you could use that gun? Fucking idiots. How dare you? What the hell did you think you were doing?

They still weren't going to say. But there was no point now. No one was going to believe them, whatever they said. Might as well not bother. Except Peter did. 'We was going to get you some pigeons, that's all. We never saw the stupid dog. Got nothing to do with us. We went out after pigeons.'

'Shut up!' She got in front of him, had him pinned up against the table. 'Shut up, you! Just shut up, shut up, shut up!' Her face was inches from his, her staring eyes, the smell of her breath. 'Who asked you to go after pigeons? Since when do you decide what's done around here?' Her voice screeching in his ears. They'd been hearing that voice since before they could remember, since before they could under-stand what she was saying. Shut up. Do this. Do that. Stupid little beggars.

Their father said, 'You'd better get lost before I belt the pair of you.'

She stepped away from Peter suddenly. Went from raging to ice cold in one moment, like she could. 'That's right. Get lost and stay lost, then we wouldn't have you round our necks. Put the kettle on, Ted, I want some more tea.'

They went. They got on the bikes and rode away. They'd go to Minehead, to the amusement arcades and she'd never bloody know, would she? Then they remembered they hadn't got any money. So they rode up and down the road for a long time and then they went and sat in a field and eventually it was beginning to get dark so they went home. Their parents were watching television. They didn't look up. 'You again,' she said. And the boys went upstairs. They hadn't had anything to eat all day but it didn't seem to matter.

'Have you any idea who could be responsible?' said Richard.

Stella shrugged. 'Someone let him out, it would seem, and then . . . I must have left the french windows unlocked.'

'Was anything taken?'

She shook her head. 'Nothing at all, so far as I'm aware.'

'Would the dog have attacked the intruder – tried to see him off?'

'Inconceivable. He welcomed one and all.'

'I remember.' Both now recalled Richard repelling Bracken's fawning approaches with irritation. 'In that case,' Richard went on, 'the shooting of the dog would seem to have been the prime intention.'

'I suppose so.'

'Surely no one from round about . . .'

'There are a couple of boys,' said Stella reluctantly. 'Sons of the people at the agricultural contractors. The parents are civil enough, but the lads are distinctly surly. Conceivably it was them. But we shall never know and I don't intend to pursue the matter.'

'How very unpleasant. I'm so sorry.'

He was, Stella could see. Quite toppled from his usual brisk application to the matter in hand. He put his tool-kit down on the kitchen table and stood looking at her. Then he reached out and held her upper arm for a moment, a gesture that she found unsettling rather than consolatory.

'It is. But I'm coming to terms with it. I mourn poor Bracken and remind myself that I've observed plenty of this kind of thing.'

'But not as a participant.'

'True. A new perspective.'

'How did you deal with hostility in Nile villages and wherever?'

'Diplomatically. One was trained to expect it under certain circumstances and react with tact and restraint.'

'Unlike real life,' said Richard.

'Oh, the anthropologist has to rise above that. Which is probably why we're unfit for it when it comes to the crunch.' Glib, thought Stella. Flip. Somehow he provokes me to be like this.

'Well, that's as may be,' he said. 'More to the point, why do you imagine these youths picked on you, if it was them?'

'Heaven knows.' She wanted suddenly to be rid of the matter. 'Just that I am in the line of fire, I imagine, or rather Bracken was. No doubt they have problems of their own. Anyway . . . enough of them.'

'Right.' He picked up the tool-kit. 'Just let me say, though, that I do think you should perhaps think of further security.'

'Handgun under the pillow? An arms race?'

'Window locks. An alarm system, possibly.'

'I'll think about it.'

'Please do.'

She watched him dismantle the mower. His concern caught her in some deep, unsuspected, vulnerable place. Those who travel alone do not often experience the concern of others.

No one nags them to take care, no one awaits them with anxiety – or reproach. Stella had thought herself indifferent. Just occasionally, a doubt flickered.

He crouched beside the machine – a spare man still, carefully fending off a paunch. You would have thought him younger, until his face in profile showed that slippage around the jowls, his bare arms displayed those ropy veins, the mottled skin. She couldn't remember with any clarity what he had been like when he and Nadine were married – there was just a dim impression of some sharper, smaller version of the man before her now. It is not true that people diminish with age – it is those earlier remembered selves who are in some way pared down, depleted, like those who look out all unaware from old photographs.

And here they were now, washed together. All because long ago Nadine joined a political association for young Conservatives: 'No, of course I'm not one, I'm not anything in particular, am I? But someone told me it's where you meet men, and frankly London is a desert as far as I can see, unless you're going to sit in espresso bars and trawl, and we're used to better than that, aren't we?' Nadine had left Oxford without any promising attachment. She was working in a desultory way as an assistant in a West End bookshop, where she received her friends and reconsidered strategy. She was twenty-three and starting to panic. The political association was nicely opportune. 'And, believe it or not, I think I've already met someone. The very first time I went to one of their dos. He's called Richard and he's at the Home Office, and he's definitely interesting. He's taking me to Covent Garden next week.'

And thus begins a lifetime in tandem, thought Stella. Extraordinary process, pair bonding. Quite as arbitrary, really, among humans as among animals. Simply a question of who happens to hove into view when the moment is ripe.

'I bet you didn't know I nearly had an official role at your wedding,' she said to Richard.

'He'll do fine,' says Nadine. She is different, tipped from girl to young woman. She is plump and creamy. The big green-gold eyes and long lashes and that satisfied pussy-cat look to her. You expect whiskers and folded velvet paws, claws sheathed.

'Love again?' says Stella.

'Of course.' But that is crisply laid aside and Nadine is off at once on a rundown of the wedding dress, the guest list, the reception at a country house hotel. 'Richard's got two little nieces who'll make sweet bridesmaids. I don't suppose you'd care to be matron of honour?'

'Well . . .'

'OK – I'll let you off.'

And in the event Stella did not even attend the wedding, because the chance arose to do field-work on a project in Cardiff with a posse of other graduate students, and thus while Nadine was parading down the aisle on Richard's arm, Stella was in Tiger Bay interrogating Lascar seamen. She was so heady with this first taste of professional fresh air – out there amid the real thing instead of stuck at a library desk – that she almost forgot to send the statutory telegram. Besides, she sensed that they were already spinning inexorably apart. She had inspected Nadine's wedding present list with bewilderment. Denby ovenware? Pyrex dishes? Coffee percolator? Travel rug? The revelation of such freight filled her with dismay. If this was the requisite accompaniment to marriage, then no thank you. In Cardiff she had a brief but charged affair with the director of the project, the stereotype charismatic older man – an appropriate and illuminating rite of passage, she felt. Nadine sent a honeymoon postcard from Majorca, hinting complacently at suspected morning sickness.

'Indeed I knew,' said Richard. 'Nadine was most put out. You were to have been got up in apricot velvet, to complement the bridesmaids.' He rose. 'There, that's fixed now, I hope.'

'Fancy your remembering. The apricot velvet, I mean.'

'It was a heightened time. Details tend to stick in the mind. I remember thinking that the colour would be becoming – with your hair. And in the end you weren't there at all. May I use your kitchen sink? My hands are filthy.'

'Of course. No, I wasn't, was I?' She had heard him with surprise. I thought he didn't much like me, back then. Disapproved slightly. Found me rackety, uncongenial. 'I was serving my apprenticeship in Cardiff docks. The apricot velvet is news to me. I rather let Nadine down, didn't I? We were already off in different directions, I suppose. Nadine always knew what she wanted and I never did. Just took what came up. Or failed to, as the case may be . . .'

She followed him into the kitchen. 'I'm sorry you've got in such a mess – there's a nail-brush on the side there. And thanks. I am grateful, even if I don't sound it. Grass cutting has never been a central concern. Indeed, I can't believe I've come to this.'

'In that sense you've led a sheltered life. It's routine for me, as a long-term householder. But I sympathize. Perhaps . . .'

'In fact,' she said, 'there's a lot that's giving pause for thought at the moment. Here am I, having put down roots for the first time ever, and supposedly a connoisseur of community life, unable to identify a community or even establish cordial relations with my neighbours. Oh, I dare say it's partly that this dog business has unnerved me. I'll make us some coffee, shall I?'

'Yes, please. So far as community goes, I can't say that I . . .'

'Oh, but you do. Beavering away for local societies. Attending church. You've slotted in. I can't manage that particular slot. And the rest are largely inaccessible by virtue of age or occupation – the farming layer, the arts and crafts enclave, the landed gentry. I can't see myself striking up an accord with the Rotarians or the Golf Club. The truth is that this place is a web, a network, it has many dimensions. The communities I know about are integrated. Concrete. They have a shape, a structure. Archetypes. Museum pieces, indeed, I suppose. No milk? Nor sugar either, right . . . The fact is, I'm an expert on systems that no longer exist. Even Tiger Bay back in the fifties was something of an entity. As for my Orkney island . . . But down here what we have is a cauldron, a late-twentieth-century melting pot. All sorts of mutually exclusive groups co-existing after a fashion. And I'm in there with the rest of them. In fact what I'm really wittering on about is myself, I think. Quite as alienated in my way as anyone else. Just as I always have been. On the outside looking in.'

Richard considered. 'That is what you were trained to do.'

'There you are, then. Unfit for real life. Or at least for any of the versions of life going on around me here. So the question is . . .'

He cut in. 'Does it matter?'

'Probably not,' she said after a moment. 'It requires a

process of adjusting expectations. Or adjusting – period. Learning to keep still.'

I suppose that's it, she thought. I have been expecting to move on, all this time. Treating this as yet another perch, from which to investigate and observe. I have not taken root at all. Tweaking at the hedge, cutting the grass – ritual gestures only. Acquisition of a dog . . . But it is the fate of the poor dog that would appear to have thrown me.

She felt entirely dispirited. The house seemed to squat on top of her, its cargo of furnishings hemmed her in. Richard was talking and she hardly heard him. He was proposing a visit to the north Devon coast. Therapy, I suppose, she thought. I have become an object of charity. Lawnmower repairs and restorative excursions. No, no . . .

' . . . and possibly the walk to the Valley of the Rocks, if we felt sufficiently energetic.'

She thanked him. What a nice idea, she said. Maybe in a week or two. I have to tidy up that article I was working on. Let's talk . . . And thank you. She saw him into his car, stood for the polite farewell. He lowered the window. 'I came with the intention – ' he avoided her eye, fiddled with the ignition key – 'anyway, it was inappropriate. The dog – I can see that has been distressing. I shall be in touch, Stella. Very shortly.'

She watched him drive away. What was that about? The uncharacteristic hesitation, the sudden opacity?

They'd killed the dog just because they suddenly got the idea. And afterwards they told each other there was no way she'd ever get to know. But she did and first she'd laid into them and now she was either lashing out or else pretending they didn't exist, setting three places at the table instead of five, ignoring them if they spoke. Making a fuss of Gran, being matey with their father.

They began to spend most of the time in the sheds. Their father was out on jobs – it was harvest now and he had contract jobs every day. The boys bashed at the corrugated iron. This shed they were making. Sometimes her face was staring up at them, staring, shouting – 'Shut up, you! Shut up, shut up!' – and then they'd bash that. Smash, bang! Now it's your turn to shut up.

Shut up and listen, they told her. You think you're so clever, you think you know everything. But you don't. We've done things you don't know anything about. We can do it again. And you'll never know. We'll do another and watch you not knowing who did it. We'll do one you can't miss.

Chapter Seventeen

When high summer arrives in the west of England the arteries begin to clog. The M5 is an oozing river of vehicles that thrusts down through Somerset to disgorge into the heartlands of Devon. The A39 crawls, day after day, clotted with caravans, trailers, cruisers. The coastal cliffs wear a mantle of camp-sites; each cove, each bay, each stretch of sand is peppered with human flesh. Anywhere with a cathedral and pedestrian shopping precinct on offer is awash. The Exmoor car-parks are spilling into the heather, there are timed visits only to Lynmouth and Lynton, a three-day waiting list for Clovelly, Cornwall was declared closed on 10 August.

But behind and beyond this surface pollution the place remains unscathed. Normal activities continue. Crops grow and are harvested. There is getting and spending, birth and death and the pursuit of love. Those who are a fixture in these parts endure and ignore as best they can. In due course the seasonal tide will ebb, leaving behind the enriching silt of its visitation. Many are nourished, some are entirely sustained. The place has learned to diversify, in tune with the times.

It has been ever thus, of course. Coleridge blazed a trail. The Victorians had a penchant for points west. The Edward-ians loved it, descending with their bicycles and their walking gear. The West Country was still quite a long way away, at the turn of the century, but getting closer all the time. Now it is no distance at all – one stop-off at Granada Services and you're there. Everyone has been west now, at one point or another, though many barely notice. But among the million birds of passage there are always those few who alight, for whom the place fulfils some need. Those who see it as a promising market stall for their craft products, those with skills to offer, those without. Those seduced by that siren scenery, those in search of a rural nirvana. Those in doubt and those, perhaps, in flight.

Stella and Nadine are having a heart-to-heart – once upon a time and long ago over midnight Nescafé in front of the gas fire in Stella's room – though there is perhaps rather more of Nadine's heart on offer than there is of Stella's. Nadine has suffered a reverse in love, but she will pick herself up, as ever, put herself together again and sally forth to fight another day. Stella is sympathetic but clear-eyed.

'I did warn you. Anyone could see it would all go up in smoke.'

Nadine stares at her for a moment.

'Anyone but me. And it wouldn't happen to you, would it? The thing about you is that you always manage to stay on the outside. You're the cat that walks by himself. You're on the edge always, looking on. Interested. But . . . detached – that's the word. You're not like the rest of us. How do you do it? One always has this feeling that you'll just take off, when it suits you.'

'The thing about you, Stella,' says Dan Mitchell, 'is that you are entirely independent. It's a great gift – and a rare one. Most people need tethers of one kind or another. They need a support base – spouses or offspring or property. They need an organization to wrap around themselves, or they need power over others, or they need adulation and approval. You seem to get by without any of that.' He props himself on his elbow and stares at her across the beach towel. She sees his face dark against the hard blue sky; there is a smell of sun oil, salt, sand and ripe melon. 'It's not a criticism – far from it. Don't get me wrong. It's not that you set yourself apart from the human race – it's simply that you seem to be self-sufficient. While the rest of the world is enmeshed with one another – which, of course, is your professional subject, a nice anachronism, by the way – you walk alone. That's what you prefer.' He is silent for a moment – then he laughs. 'And the thing about me . . . is that I suspect I'm the same. So where does that leave us, I wonder?'

'You're a strange woman, Stella,' says Alan Scarth. 'I've not known the like of you. You come from nowhere, you're beholden to no one – or so it seems. You traipse the world asking people who their grandfather married, but you carry no baggage of your own. This place fits you like a glove – I've seen that in your face all these months. But you'll not marry me, will you? You'll not settle for anywhere or anyone, will you? You're a risk-taker, but that's the one risk you'll never take.'

Letter from Richard to Stella
    My dear Stella,
       I had intended to put this to you personally rather than in a letter, but the moment was not right when I visited you last

week. And on consideration I feel that the case may perhaps be more coherently stated on paper. I trust, by the way, that you are by now getting over this unfortunate matter of the dog.

I want to suggest that we join forces. That we live together, in short. Let me set out the arguments in favour of such a venture.

PRACTICAL ADVANTAGES. One set of living expenses rather than two. My house would supply ample space for both of us – separate studies, shelving for your books easily installed. Your cottage, though charming, is somewhat on the small side even for a single person. You have mentioned a problem with the septic tank drainage system. I would propose that we pool both resources and energies – housework, cooking, etc. Shopping, incidentally, would become less wasteful – you will have noted that Somerfield, Tesco, etc., do not cater sufficiently for the single-person household. I should mention that my pension is of course index-linked – I take it that yours is also (if USS it undoubtedly will be).

There is the further point that we are both at the time of life when illness becomes more likely. The provision of mutual support has a distinct appeal.

EMOTIONAL DITTO. Solitude. I am frequently lonely. I appreciate that for you this may not be so much of a problem – you have lived rather differently. Suffice it that should you look kindly upon my proposal, I would respect your need for a degree of privacy, while hoping to convince you that a shared existence has its compensations.

PHYSICAL RELATIONS. Sex – not to put too fine a point on it. We have reached the stage when the libido is in decline. I will say simply that mine is not yet extinguished and I have always found you an attractive woman. However, I feel that at our age this need not be a central issue.

I realize that you will be surprised – startled, even – by this proposition. But not, I hope, offended. I am aware, too, that my style of letter-writing lacks emotional fervour. My trade has left its mark. I must ask you to believe that surface appearances can be deceptive, Stella.

I shall await your response with cautious optimism.

Yours affectionately,

Richard

Letter from Judith to Stella

Dearest Stella,

Look – things have come to a head. With Mary, that is. To be honest, I can't take it any longer. You've known, I'm sure, that it's not been an ideal set-up for quite a while now. I've felt as though I'm being quietly smothered. She's a super person in many ways but – well, she has to own whoever she's with and I'm just no good at being owned.

I've moved out. The only way to do it. Endless argument and recriminations otherwise. I'm in b. & b. – address and phone number above.

Now – I'll come to the point. But let me say first that I've wondered about this many times before – it's certainly not a question of any port in a storm.

What would you say to the idea of you and me setting up together?

Shock horror? Nothing physical – don't get me wrong. Just that nowadays two seems to me better than one. Despite the Mary experience. We've always got on a treat, you and me. Never a cross word. Well – hardly ever.

I haven't got much money but I can pay my way. I could doss down in that boxroom at the cottage. For the moment – if you think we might give it a whirl.

Well? Or have I shot my mouth off? If so, be candid – I'll
take it on the chin.

    Whatever – all my love,
      Judith

'Vine Cottage?' says the estate agent. 'Yes, I know it. On the
lower lane, right? Just along from the Morgan farm? Cream
stucco and pantiles? Yup, I've got it. Nice spot down there.
Quiet but not too isolated, that's what people like. Let's see
. . . you've got the Morgans and that other place the Bristol
family have done up. I sold them that – Mr and Mrs Pritchard.
Shambolic, it was, not touched for God knows how long.
Lovely job now. Then you've got the Hiscox place at the far
end. Those people . . .' He flicks an eyebrow, shoots a glance.
'We handled that sale, too – sold them the smallholding, way
back. Came from Surrey. Funny people to do business with,
I found. Had much to do with them? No, I don't suppose you
would. Fact is, between you and me, there's some background
there, know what I mean? Undischarged bankruptcy. Not that
I knew when I handled the sale – nice old chap had the place
before them, local man, been there for donkey's years – and
the money came through, though I wonder now where from.
Then a bloke came around a year or so later asking for Picton
– family by name of Picton – and it was clear enough to me
he meant them. Had some score to settle, I don't doubt.
Changed their name, see, to set up trading again. That's what
people do. No skin off my nose, anyway, but one makes a
mental note. There was all that mobility back then, mid-
eighties, everyone out to make the most of it, cash in, look
after themselves. Not that we were complaining.' He laughs –
a mite self-consciously perhaps. 'Well, it was windfalls all

round, wasn't it? For anyone who had their nose to the ground. And good luck to them, say I. You felt the ripples even down in these parts. New faces, new money, new ideas. There's been some very nifty projects in the leisure and tourism department – all strength to their elbow, given a lift to the area, hasn't it? Put us on the map. But then of course there's been others took a tumble. Swings and roundabouts, isn't it? We pick up the pieces, in my business, is how I see it. Anyway . . . to our muttons. Your property. Looking for something a bit bigger, are you? Oh – moving away altogether. We'll be happy to look after the sale for you. The market's not buoyant round here, but you've got a nice little place, shouldn't be any problem.'

Letter from Stella to Richard
> Dear Richard,
>> This letter is difficult to write . . .

Letter from Stella to Judith
> Dearest Judith,
>> This letter is impossible to write . . .

North Somerset Herald

Blaze at Agricultural Contractor's

A fire on Thursday night that destroyed outbuildings and agricultural machinery belonging to contractor T. G. Hiscox spread also to the adjoining family bungalow, causing extensive damage. The family of five escaped but an 86-year-old woman was taken to Williton hospital suffering from shock and smoke inhalation. Three fire engines tackled the blaze and a spokesman for Minehead Fire Brigade said that there was no immediate indication as to the cause. Mr Barry Smith, from

South West Electricity, who examined the site the following day, said that there was no evidence of an electrical fault. Police investigating the fire are anxious to contact Mr and Mrs Hiscox, who left with their teenage sons Michael and Peter while firefighters were still at work. Mrs Hiscox's mother remains in Williton Hospital but Detective Constable Harris said that he has so far been unable to trace the rest of the family, who have not been seen in the area since the blaze.

A CHARACTER DETACHED COTTAGE occupying a peaceful situation a mile from Kingston Florey village and with excellent views in a southerly direction.

Good-sized living-room with inglenook, kitchen/breakfast room, bathroom, bedroom, bedroom/boxroom. Pleasant gardens to front and rear.

Mains water and electricity. Septic tank drainage.

DIRECTIONS: The property lies off the B4167, going east from Kingston Florey. Access is by way of the lane to the right half a mile beyond the village (with sign indicating T. G. Hiscox, agricultural contractor).